The Fish in the Stone

EAMONN McGRATH

D1290146

THE
BLACKSTAFF
PRESS

BELFAST

The characters and situations in this novel are wholly fictitious. They do not portray and are not intended to portray any actual persons, parties or situations.

First published in 1994 by
The Blackstaff Press Limited
3 Galway Park, Dundonald, Belfast BT16 0AN, Northern Ireland
with the assistance of
The Arts Council of Northern Ireland

© Eamonn Mc Grath, 1994
All rights reserved

Typeset by Paragon Typesetters, Queensferry, Clwyd

Printed by The Guernsey Press Company Limited

A catalogue record for this book
is available from the British Library

ISBN 0-85640-524-8

for Garvan, Orla,
Fergal, Grellan, Cliona,
Ultan and Donogh

There is the man who lusts for his own flesh:
he will not give up until the flame consumes him.

Ecclesiasticus 23:23

ONE

Back to school. (Gloom!) Not talking to Denise Murphy or any of that crowd. I saw them messing with the blackboard, and when Mr Hurley moved it round on the roller, his name and mine came up and they all started giggling. He rubbed them out and pretended not to notice. But I was mortified. Even Angela smiled until I gave her a dig. Best friends — most of all, best friends — really deep down, are glad when something like that happens to embarrass you.

Nice dinner — chips and jelly. Why do they always fight? Daddy looked so sad all evening. She snaps at him and he means no harm. Watched television after homework. Love to live in America — the sun and all those sports cars. Love to have a tan and look like that girl by the pool. My face is all pimples. My left breast is smaller than my right. Wonder am I normal? Wish I had a mother like Mrs Fox. She's beautiful — always wears make-up and is so well groomed. I'd love to be grown-up and sophisticated like her, instead of being clumsy and awkward and never knowing what to do when people look at me, especially boys.

look at.

Mary closed the diary and sat dreamily with her hands supporting her face. She wouldn't always be like that. She'd travel and have adventures. She'd dance through life like a wave of the sea and be beautiful and enigmatic and be admired by men – dangerous men, experienced men of the world that would make her swoon just to look at.

Mrs Ennis was disposed to be melancholy on Fridays. Friday was the day – it would soon be two years since – poor Tom went away. He had gone without even saying goodbye. He hadn't phoned. He hadn't written. She wasn't sure where he was any more. She didn't even know whether he was still alive. She had a special perpetual novena going for him and every Friday lit a votive candle to guide him on his wilful, erratic way. He had been a sensitive and delicate child. Her love for him had always been full of pain and insecurity – bound up as it was with her fear of loss.

He was to blame. He had never taken to the child, despising him as a weakling. He had always withheld his affection from him. When he was young, he had beaten him. When he grew older, he had ignored him and excluded him from his life. Later he had stood by sardonically, watching his own son drift into dangerous ways and had done nothing to help him. Poor Tom! Because he had been innocent and weak and lonely, he had been seduced away from her into things that it sickened her to think about.

Her husband was in need of prayers. They were all in need of prayers. Prayer was something she had never succeeded in introducing into her marriage, or into family life.

They were always too busy or preoccupied. Whatever moment she proposed for prayer was always the wrong – the inopportune – moment. Without prayer you were no better than a rudderless ship, foundering in the mist. She would have to assail heaven on their behalf. She would have to make sacrifices and go on pilgrimage. Lourdes was the place to visit. She could lay her troubles before the shrine, help with the sick, and in this way expiate their offences and her own.

It was the night of her committee meeting. All through tea she had been thinking about their church gate collection. As chairperson, it was her responsibility. There was bound to be bickering. For a long time now, there had been two schools of thought. The conservatives argued that St Patrick's Young Missionary Society should be financed through the contributions of its members and through donations discreetly sought. The more radical view, to which she was partial, held that there was such dire need for priests worldwide that every means should be used to collect funds for their education. The labourers were few and the vineyard immense. Maud Feehan would object. We'll be having raffles next! she would cry in her prim, schoolmistressy voice. And why not? There was nothing wrong with raffles, or with cake sales either, if they brought in the money.

Mary would stand with her at the main gate for ten mass. She wouldn't like doing it. She never liked doing anything her mother wanted her to do, least of all standing shoulder to shoulder in public, giving Christian witness. But, as her mother, she had the right to insist. Girls of her age had all kinds of inhibitions: their schoolfriends would snigger; they would be taken for Holy Marys. She had always been a difficult child, taciturn, rebellious – jealous of poor Tom and his easy, loving ways, his rapport with his mother. When she wasn't scribbling away in her room or reading a book – but never a religious book – she was hanging on the arm of her father, wheedling concessions out of him, dressing in anorak and wellingtons to accompany him on one of his shooting expeditions, returning with snipe or pheasant, which were left hanging until they rotted and stank the place out before she was allowed to cook them.

It was typical of him to take up shooting when they were courting. No doubt he had thought that it would recommend him to her father. It gave him a squirish image and fed his conceit about being a landed gentleman. It was odd that he was the one who didn't want to part with Gortnaheensha. For her, in spite of her happy childhood there, it had become an intolerable burden. All she had to do was walk in that walled garden – once a riot of flowers and summer shade, now a wilderness of weeds – to feel her heart faint and her eyes fill with tears. The past, the lost, irrecoverable past, was her undoing. The memory of that garden as it once was, the summer breeze teasing the grass and setting the heads of tall flowers nodding, bit like acid. She could never hear the orderly sound of a rake on gravel or the lumbering trundle of a wheelbarrow without a stab to the heart, an ache in the memory. The image that recurred most often now was of the door in that wall, which she herself, in her naïveté and ignorance, had opened to James Ennis, when, in his whistling, careless way, he came pedalling up the avenue to deliver the week's groceries.

The property had been hers to dispose of and she had

sold the bulk of the land first and later the house and gardens. Her husband still went out there occasionally and Mary with him. The Patrician fathers had bought the house and he kept an eye on it for them, examining the roof for damage after storms, supervising the work of tradesmen. It distressed her to hear that the beautifully proportioned bedrooms had been divided into cubicles and the handsome marble fireplaces boarded up when central heating had been installed. The new owners had torn off the roof, and the huge Bangor slates – one of which had fallen during a gale, slicing down like a guillotine and almost decapitating a donkey – had been replaced by shiny, characterless, factory-made tiles. It was easy for him to be unmoved by it all. He had no real feel for the place.

As she stood up to prepare for her meeting she reflected on her alienation from them. They were oblivious of her departure. He was preoccupied with his accounts. Mary was leafing back through an old diary, stopping to read something she had written years ago. Caught in a loop of evening light, mellow as drained honey, they sat at ease in each other's company, exchanging smiles that went deep and found understanding, smiles that had no cognisance of her or of her needs, high-walled, unscalable smiles.

He often stood there, looking out over Paupers' Acre, thinking of her. It had been one of his favourite haunts as a boy. He had lurked and lingered among the neglected tombstones, hiding in the long grass, playing truant from school, making ghostly moans to frighten passers-by. The place was said to be haunted by the spirits of the forgotten poor who had died in the workhouse and been buried there. Neither the social implications of the place nor its supernatural terrors had ever bothered him – any more than he had been troubled by the poor suicide's strange grave that clung like a limpet to its outer wall. His mind had always been absorbed with other things, lifting him beyond the trees, where tumbling crows tore the silence into rags, beyond the fence, where the land dipped and swooped towards the town. Down there was the place where they had met – where it had all begun.

For some reason that he could not explain he had never allowed his feet to follow his mind. Every time he had stood there he had felt the same prompting, the same curiosity, the same urge to see the place again. He had even, on occasion, crossed the wall and taken a few steps over the sad mounds of Paupers' Acre, when some fear in himself, some reluctance to disturb the past, some wish to preserve just one illusion intact, made him turn back. Perhaps it was the fear that it had been just an illusion – no more than the dream of a summer's afternoon – that kept him away. Someday he would go down there again, but not yet. It was something to keep in reserve. It would be his ultimate fall-back position.

When he had woken up, she was gone. The trampled ring where they had celebrated their joy in being alive was still there. A fragrance still hung in the air, part summer, part girl. He had called to her but there had been no answer. He had climbed the ditch and looked around. Below him was the town, its narrow streets serpentining between squat houses. Nothing to be seen – no sound, no movement anywhere. Behind, the wall of Paupers' Acre rose to meet the sky. He had leaped the wall and searched for her among the tumbling tombstones. All his life since had been a search and a hope.

She had been, perhaps, Mary's age or younger – a laughing, forward girl. The memory had remained, a promise of what might be and what could be – an unsettling vision that had left him dissatisfied and unfulfilled. It had been a touchstone against which he was to measure – and find wanting – everything that had happened to him afterwards.

He turned away and went morosely down into the town, conscious of his descent into the banal and the ordinary. Mary was in the kitchen when he went in. She was sitting at the table, writing. He laid his hand affectionately on her bowed head and asked, 'Where's your mother?'

'Novena night,' Mary said, without lifting her head.

When it wasn't her novena night, it was her confraternity night or her Child of Mary night. She had a night for everything, he told himself sourly, but no night at all for her husband.

He went upstairs and down the corridor to the bedroom. His eye fell on the single bed she had set up for herself. Prim, withdrawn, like a spinster holding down her skirts, it stood in one corner – a clear demarcation line between it and the double bed on which he had thrown himself. She was a bad sleeper; his tossing about, his tendency to sprawl and elbow, woke her up; it would be better for both of them – so her argument had gone.

The compromise was typical, he felt. A less hypocritical – a more honest – person would have moved out altogether. But appearances had to be preserved. There was Mary to consider. She must not know that her parents had differences – incompatibilities. The façade of a Catholic marriage must be left intact.

That had been months ago. He was sure that the girl understood very well. She was certainly aware of the tensions between them since that time – not that it had been any better before. Her mother had never had much appetite for that side of marriage. For her it had been harsh duty and no pleasure. She had a puritanical view of what was permissible, of when and how. It was virtuous to be reluctant about such things, to hold them in contempt, to see them, at best, as a necessary evil.

When he went downstairs again, Mary was still at the table. She was leafing through a large exercise book with hard black covers. He could see that the pages were filled with neat, precise handwriting.

'I'm going out,' he said, as he passed through.

The street lamps were coming on as he slipped into Hickey's lounge. The place was deserted. He found a remote corner and ordered a large whiskey.

Sometimes she combed back through her diaries to make sense of what was happening. She had the feeling that if only she could recall everything, she would understand it and maybe – just maybe – learn how to control or shape it.

10 September 1979
Last night I woke to hear them arguing again. Through a gap in the curtains I could see the moon, round and silvery like the Host when the priest holds it up at mass. It was such a holy and peaceful thing, suspended there above the world, that I wanted to cry.

She remembered those voices – hers thin, sharp,

complaining; his puzzled, aggrieved, angered. She had put her hands to her ears to blot it out and had begun to say her prayers. She must have drifted off, because the next thing she remembered was the sound of someone padding about in the room.

She started up in fear. Someone in the room had been at the centre of her nightmares since childhood. But before she could cry out, the voice of her father whispered, 'It's all right, girl. It's only me.'

She could sense his bulk in the gloom. She got the scent of tobacco – warm, agreeable, male. He came round into the moonlight and stood there.

'I heard voices,' she said, searching for an explanation.

'Your mother . . . and I' – he sat down on the bed at her feet – 'we had words.'

He spoke in an apologetic tone. It was as if they had reversed roles – as if he was the child and she the parent. She didn't like it.

'I hate it when you argue,' she said. 'It makes me afraid.' She wanted to say that she sympathised with him, that her mother was in the wrong.

'I know, child. These things shouldn't happen – but they do.' He patted her feet in a placatory way.

She began to feel that it was nice having him sit there, taking her into his confidence. It was conspiratorial. It was against *her*. She wondered what it was like to be married and to quarrel, and what kind of a world it was when adults didn't seem any wiser or more able to cope than children like her.

'Try and sleep,' he said eventually. 'I'll sit here awhile. Let you go asleep like a good girl.'

Her mind swung back to childhood, when he had sat by

her, his hand comforting her head, while she fought her way out of the leaden grip of some nightmare. 'I want to wake,' she would scream, clinging to him. 'It's hiding behind my eyelids. It comes back when I close my eyes.' He'd wake her up fully and read her a story until her mind settled into a less compulsive groove. Then he'd sit by her, crooning softly, as she drifted off again.

She had drifted off quickly on that occasion. She had wakened later and found him lying beside her in his dressing gown on top of the bedclothes, warm and comforting as in those early years when he had taken her into their bed, while the nightmare lurked on the threshold of sleep.

When she awoke again, he was gone.

TWO

Sometimes when he looked at Mary, she was there beneath the skin, playing hide-and-seek with him. When a smile rippled Mary's cheeks like sun on windblown grass, the face became hers. The first time it happened he had been taken by surprise. Now he had grown accustomed to looking for her. Quietly, almost furtively, scarcely acknowledging to himself what he was doing, he threw searching glances Mary's way. She was in Mary's walk, in the lift of her body, in the youthful curve of her face.

He recalled again his sense of loss that day near Paupers' Acre. When he awoke, his clothes had been folded in a neat bundle near his head, and he had been taken by a deep sadness. Above, the sun still shone in a blue sky. The bent and bruised grass was evidence of their dance of discovery. But the girl herself was gone.

Pulling on his clothes, he climbed the ditch and scanned the fields. She was nowhere to be seen. Beneath him, the glint of sun on metal caught his eye. He jumped down and picked up a hair slide – a red butterfly, the size of his thumbnail, on a silvery pin. It was hers. He remembered seeing it in her hair.

He put the butterfly in his pocket and made his way home in an abstracted mood, feeling that all his life hitherto had been a sleep of mediocrity and this a coming awake into the fullness of himself for the first time. He went back the following day, but there was no sign of her. He hung about for hours, lying with his eyes closed, telling himself that when he opened them she would be there. He went away to walk among the tombstones, and came back again. Twilight was thickening to darkness when he returned for the last time. He waited until the sky was pierced with stars and a pale defensive moon raised its shield in the south-east, then went home in despondency.

He visited the place every day for a week and every day he found it deserted. There was nothing about it now – not even the depression in the grass – to tell of what had happened there. There was nothing but a corner of a field, no different from any other, where grass grew and cattle grazed and a few dark-leaved docks flourished.

A diary is like a deepfreeze, Mary thought. Things are put in fresh and come out again with the authentic flavour and taste of the past.

18 December 1979
Poor daddy looks so sad. He comes and goes like a ghost. I know he's unhappy and it's her fault.

As long as she could remember, it had been like that. There never was a time when there weren't sudden starts, shouts, banging of doors, things flung in anger. It got worse after Tom left − raised voices in their room at night, loud words at the table and then no words at all. It was about that time that her father had started to walk.

He would slip into her room and stand at the window, breathing hard. Without knowing exactly why, she had always pretended to be asleep. If the night was bright, he would draw the curtains and stare at the sky and the distant stars. Sometimes he came and sat on the bed and whispered her name. If she felt particularly sorry for him − and she usually did − she'd answer. Then he would sigh and say that he had no one to love him and ask her to kiss him. When she put her arms around his neck and her face to his, his cheek would be wet and he'd squeeze her very hard and kiss her in a way she didn't like. If she tried to push him away, he'd say she didn't love him. Then he'd get up abruptly and tuck her in and tell her to go to sleep and forget everything that had happened.

Sometimes she wouldn't hear him come in at all and would wake to find him lying on the bed with his arm around her. Usually she felt warm and safe when he came like that, the way she felt as a child when they − or rather he, because *she* never did − took her into their bed.

Last night he came secretly again.

She remembered a sweet dream in which she was floating, light as thistledown, through the universe, her arms and legs spread on a soft cloud and a pleasant warmth coursing through her. She was atingle with feeling, swooning and drifting and pulsing through space. She had awakened to a pleasant sensation in her left breast and become aware of the sleeping hand of her father. She could have moved a little to shake it off − and knew she should have − but it was so pleasant that she had let it lie there and thought of a day long gone when she might have been twelve.

She had been in the bathroom with her jumper pulled up, examining her chest to see if there was any development. She was so intent on what she was doing that she didn't hear the door opening or anyone entering, until she caught his slightly amused face in the glass. She let her jumper drop and turned round in embarrassment. He smiled, then reached out and lifted it.

'Yes,' he said, 'you're getting to be quite a big girl, aren't you?'

Then he touched her lightly and stooped to kiss her on the lips. She had never forgotten the sensation. It was exciting, but it was more than that. It made her feel a rush of emotions. She was suddenly aware that there was a world of things she knew nothing about, adult things that no one ever mentioned, things she was afraid of, yet wanted to know, things that would broaden the scope of her life, things she wouldn't want anybody – least of all her father – to know about.

She lay awake, straining to pick up sounds in the darkness. She had heard Mary's door opening and knew that he had gone in. What kind of man was he to invade his daughter's privacy like that? What was he doing in there? Carrying their differences to more sympathetic ears? Your mother doesn't understand me, would be his line. She understood him well enough. His behaviour – everything about him – was disgusting. His very presence in the room was offensive, a presence that lingered even when he was gone. There was a staleness about his wardrobe and everything in it that mirrored the sourness and staleness of their relationship. What an intolerable prison marriage was.

Disillusionment had come quickly. The horror of her wedding night, when the intimacies of marriage were brutally forced on her, was so great that a shutter had dropped in her mind, behind which she cowered, cold and unresponsive ever since. She had done her best to be a dutiful wife, had submitted to his embraces, but as the years went by, she had taken less and less care to conceal her contempt for men − all of whom were slaves of their passions.

She strained, listening, until she could hear the beating of her own pulse. What was he doing? Her eyes swam in velvet blackness. By the window there was the faintest hint of a lighter darkness where curtain and wall met. Not a sound from outside. No whisper of timber from the beams overhead. No pressure of wind on the roof. No sound except the tumult of her own heart.

She felt trapped by the limitations of her body. She had, long since, conceived a loathing for its functions of evacuation and reproduction. She felt betrayed by it and wondered how God in His wisdom could allow the soul to reside in corporate intimacy with such filth.

When the menopause came, she had welcomed the hot flushes, the drying up of her menstrual flow. She saw it as the closing of an obscene chapter in her life. On discovering that her husband's prurient interest still continued, she felt unable to accommodate him. It had always been her understanding that it was its openness to life that had rescued the act from total self-indulgence. To salve her conscience and remove from his way an occasion of sin, she set up a single bed in the corner and withdrew from him.

What was he doing? She got out of bed and fumbled darkly towards the door. She felt the colder current of air from the corridor on her face and traced her way along the wall to Mary's room. She listened. Nothing. She turned the knob and eased the door inwards. No sound – not even the sound of breathing. She found the light switch, snapped it on and blinked to adjust her eyes to the glare. He was standing at the window with his back to her. He neither turned nor made any gesture. In the bed Mary stirred lazily and sighed in her sleep. She switched off the light. 'For God's sake!' she hissed. Leaving the door open, she groped back to bed.

She knew well enough what was wrong. The animal in him was on the prowl. She pulled the blankets over her head, finding comfort in the bed's narrow confines. Would he come back and enforce his rights brutally as he had done before? There could be no peace until one of them was carried out of that room in a coffin.

All the women she knew had a similar problem. Their men either wanted it all the time or sought it elsewhere. It seemed to her that the whole male population was in a continual state of sexual explosion.

She had cycled with Angela to the sea – the sun out and hawthorn like foam on the hedges, a lark over Howard's Marsh, singing in a lift of bright air. They lay in the dunes and listened to the waves breaking and dying away to whispers, and breaking again and falling and fading, waiting for that second of absolute silence when even the stirring of the coarse grass seemed an intrusion.

They talked about school, Angela teasing, a little

enviously, though there was nothing really. Mary found the relationship as hard to encompass as the sand that filtered through her toes and fell away. It was not herself as a person he was interested in – just as a pupil, someone with a mind, ideas, ways of putting things. He encouraged her to write what she thought and felt, to have confidence in herself. The others misunderstood, or pretended to. It was their way of diminishing her, of bringing her down to earth. Was there always someone whose function in life was to do just that?

28 May 1980
Went for our first swim – coldish. Changed and lay sunning ourselves for hours. Angela says she loves the way the salt hardens her nipples. Wanted to touch mine. She's much more developed than me.

Why had she felt so different – as if a stranger was coming awake inside her – when Angela suggested that? And then so lonely, so depressed, so sad? Angela had laughed and said she liked being touched; she knew two boarders who did it together all the time. She wouldn't tell her who they were, but would, if she liked, show her what they did. Mary said she thought it was disgusting. But Angela just laughed, making her feel like a child. She always felt gauche and unsophisticated when Angela laughed like that.

Went for a run on the beach while Angela was off talking to some boys. I know why she went to talk to them. She wanted to show me she could handle a situation like that, while I couldn't. She probably talked to them about me, maybe invented stories.

Angela had built up a kind of mystique about him and her.

The more she said there was nothing in it, the more Angela believed Mary was deep and devious – and passionately committed. It had been flattering, and fun, at first, but now she was sick of it all. She hated Angela and hated school.

They hardly spoke on the way home, cycling twenty yards apart. She took the long road, up Ardcooey Hill, just to see what Angela would do. She didn't care whether she followed her or not. She knew she would. For all her pretence, she was a follower. She could always handle Angela, she was so stupid and so predictable.

When she came in, her mother, in that challenging and disapproving way of hers, wanted to know why she was so late. She told them over tea – just to annoy her – that she wanted to leave school in June. She could help her father, who was overburdened with business. Why did he work so hard? Why did he bother? Night after night she had watched him sitting there over his accounts, going through invoices and receipts, his face lined and worn, and thought she could be a help to him. She could get through the paperwork during the day and he could have his evenings. They could go for drives, maybe walk through the fields, sit in the garden and talk. *They* only talked about business. The rest was silence . . . or voices in the night.

When she dropped her little bombshell, the sound of delph and cutlery was deafening. Then her mother went all shrill and pulpity, saying it was out of the question. Her father smiled, put his hand on her head and said, 'We'll think about it.' She heard them argue explosively as she went upstairs.

She wondered why she always had the desire to annoy

and shock her mother? Why had she told her that Angela had said that one of the girls in school was pregnant? Why, when her mother was so full of going to Lourdes, had she said that apparitions were a lot of nonsense, the result of hysteria? Why, when she rebuked her, had she said she didn't believe in God any more? Maybe she didn't either – not in her kind of God anyway.

After her study for the weekend, she waited up to make tea for her father – something her mother never did, preferring to go off to bed and her long prayers. It was a lovely night. Mary walked in the moonlight in the garden while she waited.

Over tea they sat and talked, with the curtains open and the light from the pantry coming out to mingle with the moonlight – silver on gold. She felt that he was as lonely as she, as misunderstood. She listened while he told her what it was like when he was a boy. He asked if she was happy. What could she say? It would have taken a whole book to explain how she felt. One thing she knew: she was happy when he talked to her like that. She wanted to ask was he happy, but hadn't the courage. She thought she might have been afraid to find out. What could she do about it if he wasn't?

THREE

Our Lady would bring Tom back to her. She would kneel at the shrine, all night, if necessary, and besiege heaven until she felt her prayers had been heard. Our Lady would give a sign, as she had given one to Bernadette, would, at least, flood her mind with calmness and peace. She would join the candlelight procession, make herself a drop in that river of light flowing towards the grotto. Water was an important symbol in Lourdes – the waters of baptism, the waters of forgiveness, the healing waters of the shrine.

She remembered the breaking of the waters when she had given birth to her firstborn, that sweetly painful experience, so new, so moving, so binding them together in shared trauma. She had loved him from the first, this part of herself that had detached itself with a wrench and floated away. She remembered her sorrow as she felt it go, how she craved to snatch it back and be, as she had been, indispensable to it. She had loved it from that first stirring of life under her heart. She had carried its secret with her for weeks, before imparting it to anyone. What was it to him, who had planted it there so brutally, so casually? Men were indifferent to life. The voiding of their seed was all and the rest nothing.

Tom had been a sweet child, with those fair curls and eyes that detonated with such emotional power that they shattered her ability to refuse him anything. People had told her that she was too indulgent, that she had loved him too much. Well, if she had, it was to compensate for the violence of his father, who had beaten and brutalised him from an early age. Was it any wonder that he had grown up into an inadequate teenager, dependent on drugs? He had been initiated into them at school by the children of some of those drop-out foreigners, who had come into the area with their alien culture and dangerous habits. He had run away from home to live in a commune further west, where they grew food organically and smoked hash and copulated like animals.

She had pleaded with her husband to search for him and bring him home, but he had refused, saying that he had made his bed and could damn well lie on it; besides, he was over eighteen and could not be forced to return against his will.

Some day he would come back to her, purged and wholesome. How was she ever to forget the way he had kissed her on his first communion day, promising to be a good boy always and never forget his prayers? That was the best of him. That was the essence of him. Oh, God, she thought, why don't you snatch our children from us, all white and shining, where they stand with hands joined on such spiritual peaks? Never again will they be as prepared to go, never again leave us with such untroubled memories, such perfect images to console us in our grief.

Neither Mary nor her father ever talked of him. They had sufficient in themselves and in each other. They had no need of him as she had – and no need of her either. Mary had always been his child from the beginning. Even as an infant she had come between them. He had taken her into the bed whenever she cried, and she had soon learned to cry regularly. She resented their private conversations that stopped as soon as she came along. She resented their general air of conspiracy. What the conspiracy was she had no idea, but she knew that it was directed against her. She resented their sallies into the country in search of game. She resented their flushed and healthy return, smelling of grass and country lanes – their lives joined by chains of shared experience that excluded her.

So, she was going to Lourdes to pray for them all, was she? She couldn't just go because it was what she wanted to do, or because it was a worthy place to go. She couldn't go in humility to help the sick and make atonement for her own sins. She'd prefer to make atonement for theirs.

Her mother had accused her of taking his side against her. If she did, it was her own fault. She never spoke to her except to criticise. She never complimented her. She never touched her – she always seemed to have a dread of things like that. No fear of her coming into her room. She never commented on her growing breasts any more than she had warned her of her period. She had been terrified when it happened first. She had thought she was bleeding to death. No wonder she hated being a girl and smelling and leaking into her pants and having to find something – handkerchief, tissues, anything – to absorb the mess, and carrying that secret around with her all day.

The girls in school were always whispering about that kind of thing, and about boys and what they wanted to do – if you let them. They all said they'd never let a boy do . . . that. But there was always one exception, one fellow they wouldn't mind, if that was the only thing that would make him happy.

The supermarket was his province. He had designed it himself, the shelves radiating from the checkout points like the spokes of a Georgian fanlight. Every inch of shelving, every item of merchandise was observable from that focal point. He spent his day checking stock, poring over invoices, swearing at the phone system as he tried to contact suppliers.

His wife took over during the slack lunch-hour period and he went through the door marked PRIVATE and down the tiled passageway to the kitchen. His soup was waiting on the table and the rest of his food in covered dishes on the cooker. He removed his coat, loosened his necktie, opened his newspaper and sat in to a leisurely meal. During holidays and on Saturdays, Mary joined him. Afterwards, while she prepared and served his coffee and he unwrapped and lit one of the long cheroots that he favoured, they talked.

'One of these days you and I'll go for a holiday,' he promised. 'I'll get in a manager and we'll do the thing right.'

'Maybe you should get in a manager anyhow,' Mary said. 'You spend too much time out there. You should get away oftener, take it easy.'

'Maybe,' he agreed. 'And maybe we should go ahead with those plans for expansion – the ones we scrapped when your brother . . . took off.' He was aware of a certain awkwardness as the spectre of his son crowded the room and made it uncomfortable. 'The big store at the back is shelved and ready. There's only a couple of days' work in breaking through the wall. There's money to be made in a line of household utensils and bits of hardware that people always seem to be looking for.'

'I could do some of the paperwork – accounts and VAT,' Mary offered.

What harm if she were to leave school? It would be nice to have her around all day. He felt a warmth and a solace in her company that he got nowhere else, an excitement too, as if he were on the verge of discovery.

A beautiful bright day. Mary sat in the garden under the chestnut tree ablaze with loopy candles. Her mother always said it was nothing to the garden at Gortna-heensha. Gortnaheensha was Paradise before the Fall. She never remembered it except wild and in ruins, the walls bursting apart with ivy, and all those gables of what were once workmen's cottages, jays nesting and noisy among the loose stones, nettles and docks and decay.

12 June 1980
Angela came knocking with that eager look, all set for the sea. Said I wasn't going out and wouldn't be going. I'm sick of Angela and all that talk of school. I'm not having her around my neck for the holidays. Told her I was going away to walk on the great wall of China.

She felt so restless – waiting for something different. She'd love to get away and do new things. She had no experience of anything. She'd love to travel and see everything and try out everything. She'd begin by going to places that started with New – New York, New Zealand, New Orleans.

Lovely sun today. She won't let me buy the kind of clothes I want. Why is everything I do wrong?

Her mother never had had time for her. It was always Tom. Run and fetch for your brother. No, I haven't time to listen to you now. What's that, Tom, dear? Did you hear the clever thing Tom said? Was it any wonder she came to hate him? Did she hate him now? How could she? You must know someone to hate him and she didn't know the new Tom at all. She'd like to have a brother to talk to. It was her mother's fault that she hadn't. She ran herself like a wedge between them, splitting them apart in different directions.

Tom had gone and left them all embarrassed – her especially. She had pretended he wasn't really her brother. She told her friends he was adopted. She disowned him entirely. She hated him for letting them down and hated her for her grief. She was there, but her mother never saw her. She had thoughts and prayers and tears only for him. In the end Mary felt glad that he had gone, simply because it had hurt her mother so much.

Both of them lived – had always lived – in the past. For her mother it was Gortnaheensha and summer in that garden, brilliant with roses and hollyhocks. For her father it was something to do with Paupers' Acre. He would take them up there as children and sit among the higgledy-piggledy stones and show them, where the wall bulged like a cancerous growth, the grave of Mad Sullivan, who had been buried without benefit of priest or ceremony, and whom people had been told not to pray for, because of his unnatural act, but to throw stones in his direction whenever they passed by. It was easy in that mouldering place to feel sorry for poor Sullivan and to ask God to forgive him for cutting his own throat in his loneliness or desperation or whatever it was that had driven him to do it.

Marriages could commit suicide too, when one or both wouldn't do whatever was necessary to keep them alive. It was her mother's fault. Their marriage was drowning and she wouldn't hold out her hand to rescue it. She just turned her back and walked away. Mary was not supposed to notice such things – the silences, the sharp talk, the significance of that single bed. She was just a child. Nobody noticed that she'd grown up, that she was a woman. At least, her mother hadn't noticed it. She was off to Lourdes the following day to pray for everyone. It would never occur to her that she herself might be in need of forgiveness, her relationship with her family a shambles. Religion to her was a thing of rituals observed – the number of masses, novenas, rosaries she could tick off. Complete the Nine Fridays and it ensured your salvation. Mary was sick of that kind of religion.

She looked forward to the next ten days. The sun would have a chance to shine.

Mrs Ennis prepared for her journey in holiday mood. She bought herself new clothes – such a wardrobe as she hadn't bought since her honeymoon – dresses, skirts, blouses, underwear and a black lace mantilla to veil her head for the ceremonies. She reread the life of Bernadette by Franz Werfel and soaked herself in the atmosphere of innocence and wonder. It was such an inspiring story, faith triumphant over every obstacle.

She would make Tom and his return to orthodox living her priority. Our Lady would understand a mother's anxiety over a lost son. She would lay the problem of her impossible husband at Our Lady's feet also. She would pray at the shrine that he would be forgiven all his offences. Our Lady, who had experience of a very different type of man, would give him the grace to repent and prepare himself for the scouring fires of purgatory. Realistically, that was as much as he could hope for.

They travelled by bus to the airport and joined the other diocesan pilgrims there for the flight to Lourdes. The rosary began as soon as they were clear of the town. She answered devoutly, matching the fervour of her fellow pilgrims, a group of nuns and middle-aged women. She closed her eyes to the summer fields outside, her beads discreetly hidden in her palms, a faint odour of roses and miracles already teasing her imagination.

FOUR

They spent the day in celebratory mood — he in the supermarket, beaming at customers, she in the kitchen with the
windows open to the breath of summer and the susurrus
of insects from the garden. To keep cool she had changed
into white shorts and a loose top, and walked about bare-
foot on the tiled floor. To brighten up the dinner table she
had picked a few tightly cupped red roses and put them in
a long-stemmed glass in the centre. When he came in for
his meal he brought ice cream from the shop and, afterwards, sat back, savouring a long cheroot, while Mary
served him coffee.

In recognition of the fact that he had something to
celebrate, he went upstairs, shed the coat he was wearing
and put on a faded one of buff-coloured linen that he had
bought as a young man and worn every summer. It had
been lying in his wardrobe unused for years. To complete
his sense of liberation he pulled off his tie, opened the top
button of his shirt and turned the collar out over his coat.
It was a style much favoured by young men when he

himself had been young and carefree.

At tea time there was a salad and cold meat on the table and places laid for two. Through the open window he could see Mary taking the sun. She was dressed in a red bikini and lying on a rug, hands cupped under her head, sunglasses pushed up above her hairline. He stood watching her, scanning over her developing body to the lengthening child's face. A feeling of melancholy struck him, as if a cloud had passed over the sun. Before the feeling could take root, he tapped vigorously on the glass.

She unlocked her hands, sat up and waved. Then she sprang to her feet, caught up a blue top, and suspending it casually from one finger cast over her shoulder, sauntered up the garden. He watched her move in the lithe, willowy flow of youth and was a boy again in a sunny field.

She came in, smelling of Nivea cream and heat – a healthy body glow mixed with sun and crushed grass. 'Everything's ready,' she smiled.

He lifted an earthenware teapot and began to pour.

'The sun is beautiful,' she said, scooping salad on to her plate. 'I think I'm beginning to tan.'

His eyes were on her pale skin, spread so tautly over the firm flesh that it shone as she moved.

'Be careful you don't burn yourself,' he said.

'If I could get some cream on my back, I'd be all right.' She caught up a leaf of lettuce, opened her mouth and helped it in with her tongue.

He felt himself watching her in a dreamy way. It was almost as if he were somewhere else in the room, watching himself watch her. He watched himself smile and say casually, 'I'll put some on for you after tea.' He stood up, took off the linen coat and put it on the back of his chair, then opened the cuffs of his shirt and rolled up the sleeves to the elbow. 'It's close and stifling,' he said. 'There must be thunder in the air.'

He felt her eyes appraising him. 'Why don't you wear summer shirts?'

'Why not!' he laughed. 'Tomorrow you can go out to Jack Magner's and get me a couple.'

After tea he helped her to clear the table and took his stance at the sink with a tea towel. He noticed how tall she was. Her head already came to his shoulder. Soon she would be a young woman.

'Now,' he reminded her when they had finished, 'get me that cream.'

She brought the blue and white jar from the bathroom and gave it to him.

'Here,' he pointed to her shoulder, 'that's a dangerous place. I hope you haven't burned it already.' He sat her down on a chair, took cream on his fingers and rubbed it lightly on both shoulders. 'Tender?'

'It's OK.'

He felt pleased that her flesh should take so easily to his touch. 'Now the back.'

She sat on the side of her chair and opened her bikini top. The pale line across her back showed that her skin had already begun to tan. She leaned forward and held the top to her chest.

Dipping his fingers in cream, he massaged it into her back. Suddenly he was outside himself again, hearing himself say in a voice that seemed to his critical ear to be striving too hard to be casual, 'Could you drop the bra for a minute? The straps are in the way.'

There was a slight hesitation, then she straightened up and fumbled the top into her lap, covering her breasts with awkwardly crossed hands.

'That's better.' He applied the cream in broad strokes and watched the down on her skin glisten as his hands moved. 'Lift your elbows just a little.'

Again he was listening and watching from a distance, aware of excitement in the air. She adjusted herself demurely and sat with her elbows raised – her curved palms holding her breasts. As soon as his fingers moved in the dark down of her armpits he knew that what he had begun to do had changed.

'Breasts are very sensitive to sunlight,' he heard himself say. 'Did you put cream there?'

Any hint of alarm on her part would have sent him into immediate retreat. He observed the way she shook her head and made no attempt to demur or bar the way when he brought his hands around and underneath hers. They moved softly, creamily. He was aware of the change in her, of her body relaxing and surrendering to his hands. She half raised her arms and stretched herself, leaning backwards, opening her mouth in the beginning of a yawn, giving herself up to the pleasure of this new experience. He knew that it should end there, that what had happened should not be seen by her as something deliberately contrived. It was important, too, that the need he had succeeded in stimulating should, for the moment, be left unsatisfied.

She sat and smiled like someone awakening from sleep. Her top still lay across her knees and she made no effort to put it on again. He bent over to kiss her cheek, as he had often done in childhood. Her nipples, he noticed, were distended and dark.

'What you need is a sun lamp,' he said. 'Then you could brown all over. These' – he touched her breasts lightly – 'could do with a little colour.'

She looked down at her tiny, pale bosom. She did not make any move to shield or cover her breasts. In some way they had been liberated once they had been touched, seen and talked about. She crumpled her top into a ball and stood up. 'Would it be all right to lie out like this?' she asked.

'Why not! But you'd want to be careful you don't burn. How about this?' He tapped her casually on the bottom. 'Are you going to sun that too?'

She laughed.

He noted the laugh, weighing its composition and content carefully. There was nothing of alarm or reprimand in it.

'If you don't hurry, the sun'll be gone.' He joined in her laughter.

'Aren't you coming, too?'

'I might sit under the apple tree for a while.'

He watched her carry out his newspaper and leave it on the garden seat in partial shade – the chequered pattern of leaves and light making the wooden bars slip and slide. He lit a cheroot, picked up his glasses and followed her out. He sat in dappled ease and smoked his cigar. On a plaid rug, at a little distance, Mary lay on her back and offered herself to the sun.

When she changed position he gave a start and plucked back with a guilty jerk his dangerously adventuring imagination. He opened the newspaper. Pictures of a lunch-time crowd in Stephen's Green – ducks on sparkling water, young bodies sprawled on the grass. The sun bred relaxation, indiscretion, revelation – disrobing on the beach – skirts that lifted. How could a man be blamed? he thought.

He looked down at Mary. Her eyes were closed against the light. What was going on in that child's head of hers? He knew that what he was contemplating was wrong. There was still time to draw back. No real harm had been done yet. He mopped his forehead in the oppressive heat and listened; in the abnormal stillness a murmur of muted thunder trembled on the evening air.

14 June 1980
Quiet house. Our Lady of Lourdes pray for us! Lying out in the sun all day. Like the smell of cigar smoke. Summery in his new coat. Feel different, restless, excited. Feel I could stay up all night.

Her mind was full of new ideas, new emotions, new ways of seeing. She would need a whole new vocabulary to round up her whirling thoughts and pen them in. She closed her eyes dreamily. She felt like poetry. She felt like music. She felt strange echoes in the air, waiting to be picked up and identified. She felt – it took her a while to find the word – creative. She wanted to explore feeling. She wanted to impose order on things. She wanted to hack something clean and shining out of the general murkiness of life. She wanted to hold up a little bit of experience and polish it and shape it until it was itself – whole, one, perfect.

It was hard to know what to think. *She* – that other one – was strange. *She* liked him doing . . . that. It was exciting, and scary, when she was around. That one wanted things Mary never knew anyone could want. She thought, acted, felt differently to her. She was unpredictable. She frightened her. He was new too − different. Mary was not sure she wanted to continue.

Twilight. The sky rich and plummy, a translucent shine over deepening puce. Though the window was open, the air was hot and still. Not a breath stirring. It was as if nature was waiting for something dramatic to happen, something to cut through the heat and the silence. A summer shower, a downpour, an outburst to cool and quench was what she needed − the rush of water in chutes, wet fingers on the windowpanes, the sounds of dry earth drinking in the moisture. She wanted to feel water lukewarm but cooling on her skin. She was on fire deep inside. Her face was burning. She was like hot metal.

As she stepped into the shower the spray hit her and she felt it sizzle and spit and vaporise.

It was after midnight when the storm broke. He had gone to bed to distant muttering and lances of light on the horizon. He awoke to a crack as sharp as the splitting of the roof over his head and the deep roll of thunder, reverberating to a silence − a silence so hushed that he had to strain to catch it. He waited for the blinding flash and began to count − one . . . two . . . three. Overhead the silence shattered in a fearful rending that swelled and expanded into a deafening crescendo that overwhelmed him like the collapse of giant masonry. The bowl of the night sky was a vast echo chamber that boomed with power and devastation.

He heard a frightened tap-tap-tap on his door and

Mary's voice asking if he was awake. He called to her and heard the door open and the padding of her bare feet on the carpet. There was another vivid flare and the padding became a soft rush. For an instant he was aware of the young body outlined through the thin cotton of her nightdress, the frightened child's face. Then it was dark again and the thunder was upon them, closer, louder, more threatening than before. With a cry of terror she threw herself on the bed. He held her to him, soothing her, calming her, talking to her as he had done in childhood, sheltering her with his arms, smoothing her hair, touching it with his lips. He lifted the bedclothes and drew her in beside him. She lay into him, her body shivering and strangely cold.

Overhead there was a cool, rushing sound, then the hammer of hailstones on the roof, followed by the softer drum of rain.

'Is it over now?' she whispered.

'Yes.' He stroked her hair. 'It's all right now.'

The rain came in torrents, clogging the chutes to over-flow, beating in sheets against the wall and cascading onto the ground below. Thunder still rumbled with subdued menace in the distance, growling throatily as it paced about.

'It might come back,' she said.

'What harm if it does! You're safe here.'

'Can I stay?'

Of course. Hadn't she always come to him when she was afraid? How often in childhood had she called out for him in the darkness, or, fearful of some nocturnal noise, rushed into the warmth of their bed, where he had set her mind at rest, until she had lapsed into sleep, sprawled softly between them? Did she remember? Yes, she remembered. She'd sigh and stretch like a contented kitten and in a few minutes she'd be asleep, a warm bundle in the cold no-man's-land that constituted the largest part of that marriage bed.

'It's so cosy,' she said, 'to lie here and listen to the rain.'

'It's like old times,' he said.

He lay and watched the sheet lightning flash and fade, while the thunder rumbled intermittently and fell away into a far murmur no louder than the closing of a door in an abandoned room. Long before it died away, she was asleep, breathing noiselessly beside him.

His hand slipped down to cradle the curve of her bottom and slide over her flank. He touched her breasts, the nipples limp and sunken in sleep. She moved and her face came close to his. He bent to kiss her and felt her breath warm on his cheek. His lips brushed against the corner of her mouth, soft, delicate, feminine. He held her in a flow of unaccustomed emotions. It was a precious, sacred time to him and there was nothing in it that he would acknowledge as evil or sordid. Her body fed a hunger that had waited so long for relief its satisfaction brought tears to his arid eyes. He kissed her cheek again and then her sleeping mouth. For the first time in his adult experience his lips touched flesh that did not flinch or harden against his approach. With a sleep-laden sigh, she nestled into him, trusting, secure.

It was daylight when they awoke, yawning and stretching. The sun had already traversed the ceiling and was creeping like a honey stain down the wall. They looked at each other and smiled a slightly bemused smile at finding themselves together like that.

'Did you sleep well?' he asked.

'Yes,' she yawned. 'The last thing I remember was rain on the roof. Was there any more thunder?'

'A little.' He touched her hair and smiled. 'It's nice having company.'

He watched her eyes turn to the single bed, neatly made up at the other side of the room.

'Time to get up, I suppose.' She stretched lazily and slipped out onto the floor. He watched her raise her arms in a yawn and her nightdress move up her body and slide down again.

'Why don't you bring in your things and dress here so that we can talk?'

She turned and smiled at the door and in a minute was back again with a bundle of clothes.

He pointed to the dressing table. 'Bring over that brush and I'll do your hair.'

She sat on the edge of the bed while he drew the brush through her hair. 'That's nice,' she said. 'I remember you used brush my hair when I was a little girl. You always made a game of it and never hurt me – not like . . . ' She stopped, her eyes fixed on the bed in the corner.

He sighed and continued brushing. 'The pity is that we give up doing things like that. We say you're getting too big or too old. Maybe we never get too old for the loving thing and the caring thing. What do you think?'

'Maybe,' she agreed.

When her hair was brushed, he turned her around, letting his hands caress her warm skin.

'Did anyone ever tell you that you're growing up to be a beautiful girl?'

She shook her head, pleased and flattered, and did not

shrink from him when he took her by the shoulders and kissed her on the mouth.

15 June 1980
Terrified of thunder and lightning. Always have been. Remember hearing of a man in Galway struck down in a field on a summer's day. His body was charred to a black lump. Read in the paper this morning of sheep and cattle being killed, trees and power lines down.

It had been just like old times – so cosy and so comfortable that she almost wished the storm would get worse, because she could, maybe not exactly enjoy it, but appreciate the majesty of it, knowing that she was safe.

The days were so different. She loved the change of routine, the happy atmosphere in the house. The hostility, the whiff of sermonising and disapproval, was gone. She felt like rushing out and taking the sun and the sky and the whole world into her arms.

FIVE

He was conscious of her every movement when he came in to dinner. The room was full of her youth and vitality. Her laughter was as prodigal as the splash of sunlight on the wall. There was a rapport between them that made speech redundant. It seemed to him that they were both merging together and becoming part of the bright, brilliant day.

The magic continued after tea and through the evening. There was talk of going for a drive, but they never did. Instead, they sunned themselves in the garden – she creamed and topless on a rug, he sitting under the apple tree in a short-sleeved shirt she had picked out for him in the morning.

When the sun dipped low and eddies of wind played on the leaves overhead, they went indoors and watched television. Mary sat in her mother's chair with a light top drawn loosely over her shoulders. Occasionally they looked at each other and smiled. Later she made tea and brought two mugs and a plate of biscuits into the sitting room. They drank the tea in an easy silence. After washing up, she touched her lips to his cheek.

'I'm going to bed now. I hope there'll be no more thunder.'

'What harm if there is,' he said. 'Can't you come in with me?'

His heart leapt when she said, 'Maybe I will.'

He heard her go upstairs and down the corridor to the bathroom. There was an interval before he heard a more distant door closing, and then silence. If she had gone into her own room, it would be wiser to leave her undisturbed. Whatever he had in mind – and he resolutely refused to face up to what that might be – it could not be achieved crudely or precipitately. It would have to come naturally; it must be – or seem to be – as innocent of its destination as water sliding towards a precipice.

When he reached the door of his room he was aware of the painful constriction, of the boom and falter, of his heart. She was sitting shyly in bed with a magazine in her hand and she looked up and smiled as he came in. He sat on the edge of the bed until he had regained his composure, then took his pyjamas to the bathroom and changed there. He was determined to avoid anything that might alarm or embarrass her.

When he came back he put away his clothes in the wardrobe, and slowly, almost absent-mindedly, eased himself into bed. He lay on his back and watched the curtains move in a light sway of air. He was conscious of street sounds – a car accelerating in the distance, a lonely dog barking, passing voices. After a while she laid down her magazine and yawned.

'Sleepy?'

'Ye – es.' She played the word like a concertina.

He reached out and switched off the bedside lamp. Through a gap in the curtains he saw the blue glow of the summer night. He turned towards her and lay on his side, watching the dark outline of her head on the pillow.

'I hope you didn't get too much sun.'

There was no reply. She was already asleep.

He lay there for a long time listening to her quiet breathing, his hand straying tentatively. He loved the velvety texture of her skin.

She twitched and came awake. 'It's hot, isn't it?' she said.

'Maybe you'd be cooler in your own bed?' he said, testing her reaction.

'It's fine here,' she yawned carelessly.

'I'll throw down a blanket. Is that better?'

'Yes.'

He laid his hand on her thigh. 'I hope you haven't got too much sun. Does that hurt?'

'No.' Her voice sounded normal – without reservation or protest.

His fingers moved over her breasts. 'Well?'

'That doesn't hurt at all,' she told him. 'It's . . . nice.'

He seized the opportunity and built on it. 'Nice, is it? That's nature's way of telling you that your body is maturing and getting ready for . . . adult experience. Did you know that?'

'No,' she said.

'Girls should understand their bodies and not be ashamed of them. You're not ashamed of your lovely body, are you?'

'No,' she said again, in what he judged to be a doubtful whisper.

'Good. You should feel pleased with it, rather than ashamed of it or shy about it.'

'Yes.' The answer came hesitantly. She caught the hem of her nightdress and pulled it down. 'I feel very tired. I'd like to go to sleep.'

He leaned over and kissed her on the cheek. 'Goodnight . . . love.'

'Goodnight, Dad,' she said and turned away.

Dad. Was there deliberate rebuke in that word? Something in the tone bothered him, too, or was it just his imagination?

16 June 1980
Can't write today about the things I'd normally want to write about − the sun, the weather, the holidays, and she away.

That other one frightened her. She was foreign, strange, exotic − always wanting to experiment, to go that step further.

When she went upstairs to change into her bikini, there *she* was, standing naked before the glass. Mary watched her. She wanted her to go away and never come back.

After tea they went for a drive, looping down through the low hills to the coast. Avoiding the more frequented beaches, they came by way of meandering grassy lanes, by snug farmhouses, set gable-end to the Atlantic, and finally on foot down a fenced path to a deserted cove with high headlands on either side, where a frothing net of white water broke on a sandy beach.

They found a slab of flat rock, and while she lay shading her eyes against the westering sun, he sat — his back propped against a smooth outcrop — and watched the rise and surge of water. The cove was like a natural amphitheatre, catching and magnifying the thunder and sudden silence of the receding wave. He watched the crests form and the sidelong race of foam as they broke and tumbled and spread until they were soaked into the sand.

After a while Mary went behind a rock and emerged in her bikini. He watched as she raced down the sand and plunged her feet into the foam. She waded out, her legs growing shorter, until she stood thigh deep in flecked and broken water. She poised a moment, hands joined as if in prayer, then dived into an incoming wave that crashed and opened out around her. Somewhere in the middle of swirling water he picked out her dark head. He stood up and hurried down the beach, relaxing his pace when he saw that she was swimming parallel to the shore. She waved and shouted something as he reached the water's edge. He could not distinguish the words over the tumult, but it was clear that she was enjoying herself. He kept pace with her as she leaped and plunged and spread herself like a leaf on the water.

When she had tired of it she came back laughing and splashing, and ran up the beach ahead of him. He reached the rock as she was wiping her face with a towel and smoothing back wings of wet hair. She smiled at him and shook her hair out as he took the towel and undid the strings of her top. Gently he dried her, dabbing at her cool flesh with the soft towel. It seemed to him she responded as unselfconsciously as she had in childhood.

She took the towel from him and turned away to remove

the lower half of her bikini. He watched the interplay of sun and shade on her body as she towelled. The contrast between the tawny, grained surface of the rock, against which she stood, and the smooth perfection of her skin, warmed by the mellow evening light, worked powerfully on his imagination. He watched closely as she pulled on her pants, then he took the towel again, and kneeling in front of her, dried her feet.

With a suppressed groan, he dropped the towel and moved away. He sat, consumed with longing, and watched as she dipped her bikini into a pool to wash off the sand. She wrung it out and spread both pieces on a rock. Speared by the lengthening rays of the sun, she picked up a finger of driftwood and poked at a scurrying crab in the pool. It stopped in a flurry of sand. She touched it and stood laughing as it darted under an overhanging ledge. She set the stick floating on the surface and, seated on the rock, navigated it with her toe. Nothing that she did was too small to excite his wonder and feed his infatuation.

On their way up the narrow track they stood aside to let two lovers pass. The young woman had a laughing, open face. The young man carried a sweater over his shoulders, its sleeves loosely knotted about his neck. Ennis looked back and saw them stop to kiss where the path dipped sharply. Their feet were poised above the outgoing foam, their heads caught in a noose of light.

In bed he kept his distance, though greatly tempted by her nearness. She fell asleep quickly and he lay there, listening to the muffled noises of the night. When she turned towards him, his body trembled. Behind him was the barren past. Ahead, nothing but emptiness. No man, he raged, could be expected to go on that way.

He had heard of desperate men of his own age taking their own desperate way out. He had heard of others who had slipped off, leaving all their earthly possessions behind to compensate a bitter wife and unforgiving children. If Mary went with him, they could seek anonymity in some foreign city where people minded their own business.

He turned towards her as towards a lifeline. He held her to him fiercely; all he wanted from her was love. There was nothing wrong in that, he told himself. But the love of a daughter was not enough. What he wanted, what he needed, was the love of a woman.

Later, in that twilight land between sleep and waking, he found her body responsive to his hands. She stirred beside him, opening herself to feeling – her mind, perhaps, caught in a labyrinth of dreams that centred on her own body. Shamelessly he stimulated it, until, with a little whimper, she drew herself together, before relaxing with a long sigh.

She fell asleep immediately, settling in beside him with a drowsy purr. He lay there in a kind of exaltation, his arm about her. With patience, he told himself, it would be possible.

Another day of magic and rapport. Another night of rich opportunity, and then it happened. With feather touch he fanned her beyond caution, until he heard her sharp intake of breath and entered her. He was not aware of any feeling of guilt.

Who would have thought that it could have come about

so – yes – so naturally? There was no other word, he felt, to describe what in the eyes of society had always been considered an unnatural act. People who used words like that were indulging in legalisms. There was nothing in all his sexual encounters with his wife that had anything of the natural about it when compared to the spontaneity of this. Yet his marriage had the blessing of church and state. The law and religious canons were imprecise instruments. They legislated for an ideal world that didn't exist. The only authoritative law, as he saw it, was the law that was tailored to the individual need.

The puritan concept that had been imposed on his marriage was unnatural. The relationship, he told himself, need not be one of shame, of appetites that were better repressed, of acts that demanded apology as soon as they were indulged in. The greater virtue was not in self-denial. It was in frank enjoyment of the pleasures of the body. The sin was in the withholding of self. The sin was in the rejection of an essential part of what it meant to be human.

He had expected some reaction from Mary – shock, retreat – but there was nothing. Perhaps it had been the timing. It had come at the precise moment when nature demanded it. But what would she feel when she had time to consider? In the eyes of society what he had done was vile, wicked, inexcusable, a crime punishable by the courts. Only, that wasn't the way it had been at all. He rejected the world and its stupid, arbitrary rules, its caveats and its sanctions.

Sometime during the night it happened again. Imagination ripened into reality and dream became flesh. Then, down, down, down, into a well of warm oblivion.

When they woke it was light, a sober, respectful light,

darkly veiled. He looked at her warily to gauge her mood, unsure of what he might find. She stretched herself and smiled – bleary, a little self-conscious, but a smile. She pressed her fists into her eyes and yawned.

'Sleep well?'

'Like a log.'

This was reassuring. So that there would be no misunderstanding, he probed in his oblique fashion.

'Better than your own bed?'

'Yes.'

'That's fine!' he exulted. 'That's great! There's just one thing: you must never tell anyone about this. They wouldn't understand. Promise?'

'I promise,' she said.

It rained steadily all morning, with water singing in the downpipes and gurgling into drains. By noon it had eased off. A westerly breeze rattled up, sweeping clusters of drops off trees and flattening them into discs of light as they fell. Later the sun emerged, the breeze bundled off and little wisps and plumes of steam stole like ghosts across the grass.

He sat by the open window with his cheroot after tea and watched. The heads of the taller flowers were heavy with moisture. He looked at the dark head bent over her notebook. She lifted her face in thought and tilted it, her teeth nibbling at the end of her pen.

She's beautiful, he told himself fiercely, and she's all mine.

It had been a fast-forward, rainbow-flashing dream – a runaway rollercoaster that spun her off, after wringing from her feelings so private that she wouldn't wish any person to share them.

That shameless one had whispered to her that she must float with the warm tide, that all the things she used to think disgusting were beautiful. He had been so apologetic – and that at a time when she'd have done anything for him. He was so lonely. He had nobody to understand him except her. His wife had abandoned and betrayed him. She had turned marriage into a dungeon in which he had rotted for years.

Afterwards Mary began to wonder if she hadn't opened a door into darkness – a door that could never be closed again. The other one was so sophisticated, so reckless. She was like the bad girl in school stories, who did everything to shock and laughed at people's embarrassment. Part of her was fierce, yet part of her was soft and yielding – full of a wild submission that spread through her like fire.

It was still June. A day still had the same number of hours. But everything had changed. She was in some kind of parallel world, whose values were not the values she was used to. What was to happen when her mother came back? All the other one felt about her return was a kind of excitement at the prospect of confrontation. As for herself, it was something she didn't want to think about.

SIX

Mrs Ennis was on fire with religious zeal when she return-ed. She had responded to the atmosphere of Lourdes – a very palpable thing, in spite of the gross commercialisation – with enthusiasm. She had thrown herself into the exer-cises, the visits to the grotto, the candlelight processions. She had come back with the conviction that the future of the world depended on saying the family rosary. She had come back determined to be more charitable, more tolerant of human frailty. She had prayed for her husband at the grotto, and she had discussed his ways with an understan-ding priest, who had heard her confession.

She was relieved to find him so cheerful, even if it was ridiculous to have dug out that linen coat again. The shirt was also a mistake. The style was too youthful for a middle-aged man. There was something else about him that she couldn't quite fathom. He was more jaunty, more genial. He seemed more willing to please. He had listened patiently while, in the first flush of enthusiasm as they sat around the tea table, she described Lourdes and the impact it had made on her. He had resisted any temptation to scoff. He had accepted the rosary she brought him. He had even opened the little leather case and taken it out and examined it and murmured, 'Very nice.'

When she asked how they had fared he had smiled and looked at Mary who smiled back and said, 'Fine.' There was something exclusive in those smiles that alerted her to undercurrents and reminded her of the shoals through which their marriage had always drifted. She looked from one to the other a little uncertainly. She had no need to be told that they had probably got on very well without her.

'What have you two been up to?' she asked Mary when they were alone.

'What do you mean "up to"?' Mary parried defensively.

'He's different – sort of excited – like a boy.'

'I don't know what you mean.' Mary sprang up, ready to leave the kitchen.

'That ridiculous shirt! It's far too young for him.'

'I think it suits him very well. He's not that old.'

'He's a middle-aged man of fifty-one. Where did he go or what did he do when I was away?'

'You'd better ask him.' Mary made no effort to hide her animosity.

'You've changed too,' her mother accused. 'You're giddy and jiggy – just like him. I suppose the two of you didn't say a prayer when I was away?'

'Fifty-one isn't old.' Mary ignored her. 'It may be ancient for a woman. But a man is as young as he feels.'

It was natural, she supposed, that a closer relationship had grown up between them in her absence. She had plenty of opportunity to monitor the change over the following days. The most significant thing was that there was a kind of dangerous gaiety loose in the house. He was unusually cheerful and Mary was both excitable and disobedient. He made silly jokes at which she laughed inordinately.

Regularly he took her on drives to the sea or the country-side. When she insisted on going too, they either sat in the car and let her walk the beach on her own or they took to the fields, over stone walls and ditches that she couldn't scale. An hour later they would come back from some different quarter altogether, flushed and laughing, without apology or explanation.

However, there was one good that came from it all. He seemed to have accepted her own right to sleep alone. He never once complained about it, or made it the subject of midnight argument, and he never again used it as an excuse to seek sympathy in Mary's room.

The change in Mary was just as pronounced. Ten days before, she was little more than a child. Now she was like an adult – self-sufficient, arrogant, contemptuous even, full of grown-up assurance, and, above all, hostile. There had always been an element of secrecy about her. She had never wanted to talk or share confidences. She had never been comfortable when the two of them were left alone together and was always withdrawing, always in transit. Now it was enough for her mother to enter any room Mary was in to make her gather her things and slip away. She seemed to spend a great deal of her time in the bathroom or locked in her room. She was forever experimenting with lipstick and eye shadow and painting her fingernails. In the ensuing rows he always took her side, excusing and condoning every excess.

On Mary's sixteenth birthday, early in July, an elaborate card came for her in the post. It was so large that the postman couldn't get it through the letter box and rang the bell. Mrs Ennis took it from him and was examining it curiously when Mary snatched it from her, crying, 'That's for me,' and ran upstairs with it. Later in the day, when Mary was busy elsewhere, she had gone into her room and seen it standing on the dressing table. It was one of those sickly adolescent things – all hearts and flowers and satin ribbon. When she looked inside she saw the words 'From your secret lover' written on it. She was rearranging it on the dressing table when Mary burst in.

'You're horrible,' she shouted. 'You've no right to read my private things like that.' She held the card to her chest.

'More of your romantic nonsense,' her mother said dismissively and swept from the room. The girl was getting harder and harder to understand. Why would she send herself a card like that? She was certain that Mary had sent it. One glance at the handwriting had satisfied her of that.

Later she went into her own bedroom and found the words 'Love flowered in the desert' scrawled in lipstick across the mirror. She cleaned it off crossly and on her way downstairs went into the bathroom, where a similar scrawl proclaimed 'He loves her not.' This was the beginning of a rash of scribbles all over the house that lasted for days.

It was obvious that her father had given her money and indulged her when she was in Lourdes. There was that scandalous bikini she had on, flaunting her flesh in it about the house. There was the row of knickers, which as a good Catholic parent she had felt obliged to rip from the line and burn in the empty grate – the kind of things street girls wore. She had summoned Mary down from her scribbling and admonished her, while the flimsy things melted and blackened. Mary had stood with grim face, watching them burn. Then she had turned on her heel and rushed upstairs. Determined to have her say, her mother followed her. Mary's room was empty but the door to her own room was ajar. Mary was standing by the single bed, tearing off the blankets.

'What are you doing?'

'Getting rid of this!' Mary hissed. 'Someone should have done it long ago.'

She watched as Mary wrenched at the sheets and threw them in a corner, then stooped to lift the bed and turn it over on its side.

'Stop it!' she said.

'You're the one who's always preaching,' Mary said. 'Tell us this, then: what have single beds to do with marriage? No wonder this house is the way it is.'

Her mother was suddenly very angry. It seemed to her that she understood, at last, what had been going on when she was away. Her husband had taken the opportunity to poison the girl's mind with his own biased version of their life together. She caught Mary by the wrist and in a fury boxed her about the ears, until she retaliated by pulling at her hair and screaming, 'I hate you. You're mean and miserable and, in spite of all your pious ways, there's no religion or love in you at all.'

She pushed the girl from her and rushed in tears from the room. She was shocked by the violence she had discovered in herself, and dismayed by the harsh and scornful attitude of her daughter, who went around for days churlish and defiant, with a superior look on her face, as if she had secret knowledge that gave her some advantage over her mother. It was clear that she had inherited the character and temperament of her father and, like him, wanted to humiliate and ostracise her.

They had rearranged their lives, making decisions that would affect the future of them all, without bothering to consult her. There was that wrong-headed decision to leave school and keep the accounts. When she had challenged him about it he had shrugged his shoulders and said, 'What's the use of forcing her if she doesn't want to?'

The other one came and went now very secretly. She was often there in disguise and nobody knew about it – not even her father. A funny thing about her: she liked excitement and a whiff of danger. There were times when she wanted to claw her mother's eyes out. There were times when she wanted to tell her everything, to taunt her, to defy her. She wanted to shout, Look what you've done to him. It's you who drove him to this.

10 July 1980

A big fuss about school. Sick of school. Most of the girls don't like me. They have their own cliques and come from the other side of town. All the girls around here, except Angela and Triona, go to the community school. They've all got boyfriends from the school and go disco dancing together and think people like me who go to the convent snobbish. I hate that uniform. I hate Mrs Freaney – her teeth chewing her lower lip like a rabbit as she gives out. I'm too old for all that now. They're only kids, talking kids' stuff all the time. They and their secrets! They've never had anything worth making a secret of in their lives.

Sunday had become an important day for him. His wife got up at seven thirty to walk to mass at eight. As soon as her footsteps had dwindled on the pavement he was knocking on Mary's door. He went in and lifted her out of bed, hot and filmed with sleep, and carried her to his room to lie passively in his arms.

He would try to stimulate her into active participation or, failing that, he would take her impatiently. Afterwards there were treasured moments as he held her, listening for that quick tap on the concrete. When it came, Mary leaped out to put on her dressing gown, and when her mother came down the tiled passage to the kitchen – virtuous and superior after prayer – she would find her sleepily slapping delph about or nibbling from a packet of breakfast cereal.

Things continued in this way until the day came when Mary sought him out in a panic. The time for her period had come and gone and nothing had happened. He questioned her sharply about dates and told her to try to calm herself and, above all, not to say anything to her mother. He spent a very uneasy afternoon pacing between the shelves. When the supermarket was momentarily empty, he went inside to ask if she was sure. Her face looked pale, as if she had been crying. She could not be sure of the exact day, but it was certainly overdue. He soothed her with what he felt were hollow reassurances. It was too early to rush to conclusions. They must have patience and wait. If the worst happened, he would look after her. She must leave everything to him.

He returned to the supermarket and tried to push it to

the back of his mind. The evening was bright and sparkling, the air full of drifting pollen and the smell of cut
grass. Talk was all of holidays and the seaside, Sunday
trips into the mountains, package tours to the Costa del
Sol. He could imagine what those women with their in-
quisitive eyes and their narrow certainties would have to
say about it if they knew. What secrets did they themselves
carry behind those heat-flushed faces? Whatever was there
– and he understood enough about human nature to
know that there would be something – it would not prevent them from condemning him.

When his wife came out to help during the busy period,
he could hear her talking about her visit to Lourdes and the
wonderful spiritual experience it had been. They would
sympathise with her. They would condemn the girl – pity
her, maybe, but condemn her all the same. She would not
be fit company for their daughters, certainly not for their
sons. She would have to be protected.

A week later her period came. When she ran to tell him,
he hugged her and felt the breeze of summer disperse the
bleakness in which he had been locked. It had been a close
call and he was determined that nothing like it should ever
happen again. It had been foolish of him to take such risks.
It was a measure of his bewitchment that, until it happened, he had not allowed himself to look beyond the
deed to its consequences.

It was his custom on Wednesday afternoons, when the
supermarket was closed, to call on wholesalers in the city.
He had heard of a consultant there who specialised in
family planning. She would be safe in his hands. It was a
simple thing to make an appointment. He explained his
scheme to a reluctant and frightened Mary and coached

her in the role she would have to play.

When Wednesday came they parked by the river and walked up the steep street, past Georgian houses with rows of brass plates and expensive cars parked outside. They found the plate they were looking for, ornate and highly polished, beside an open door that led in under an ornamental fanlight to a hallway, where a second door faced them. They went in and found themselves in an empty waiting room, with a thin woman typing behind a glass partition. She looked up as they entered and consulted an appointments book at her elbow.

'Mr . . . Wallace?' she enquired, running a fingernail along a line.

'Yes.'

'Will you take a seat, please. Doctor is engaged at the moment.'

They sat down on two straight-backed chairs with padded horsehair seats and waited. He saw Mary looking at him nervously and smiled back at her.

'Remember, now,' he whispered, 'your name is Mary Wallace.'

After about ten minutes a young woman came out, settled her account at the glass partition and left. Telling Mary to stay where she was, he approached the partition and whispered to the receptionist. She lifted the phone, spoke a few words and listened.

'Yes. Doctor will see you first, Mr Wallace, and then your daughter.'

The consultant, a tall, spare man with greying hair and a grey pinstripe suit, came forward like a stooping crane to shake hands. Smiling, he pointed Ennis to a seat and sat down behind his desk.

'You have a problem, Mr Wallace,' he invited gently, 'or, rather, your daughter has a problem?'

'Yes,' Ennis said and hesitated.

'I see a lot of young women with problems,' the doctor encouraged. 'What age is she?'

'A little over sixteen. She's not . . . a virgin any more.'

'I see. You mean she's been having a relationship?'

'Yes.'

'Have you discussed it with her? Have you tried to dissuade her?'

'Yes, but' – he made a helpless gesture with his hands – 'you know what young people are like today.'

'I know,' the doctor sympathised. 'What about her mother?'

'Her mother is . . . dead. So, you see my difficulty, doctor?'

'What do you want me to do?' The doctor was abrupt but not unsympathetic.

'I'm afraid she might become pregnant.'

The doctor picked up a pencil and drummed with the butt of it on the desk. 'I see. Contraception may not be the ideal solution for problems like this. But it's preferable to pregnancy.' He looked across the desk at him shrewdly. 'You realise, I suppose, that by putting her on contraceptives we are encouraging her to continue with this relationship?'

It was a sharp observation and so near the nub of the matter that Ennis felt a flutter of panic.

'I realise that,' he said cautiously, 'but I'm convinced she's going to continue, anyhow.'

'Well, if she's determined to be sexually active,' the consultant said, 'it's advisable that she be put on the pill.

We may have to experiment a bit before we find one that fully suits her. There are side effects, you understand – headache, nausea, depression, a tendency to put on weight and, perhaps, others. The reaction can vary enormously from person to person. But we'll find the right one for her.'

'Whatever you think, doctor,' he said deferentially.

'Now, I'll see the young lady herself.'

The consultant got up from behind the desk with his hand outstretched, a professional smile like a mask on his face. 'Goodbye, Mr Wallace.'

'You'll be easy with her?' he asked. 'She's very shy, and ashamed.'

'My business is medicine, not morality,' the consultant said. 'But I will have to warn her of the dangers of promiscuity. Has she been told about venereal diseases?'

'No. I'm afraid not.'

'She'll need to be if she's sexually active. Leave it to me, Mr Wallace. I'll put her in the picture. It may be the very thing to deter her from further activity.' His smile was intended to be reassuring.

'Your bill, doctor?' he enquired in some embarrassment.

'My secretary will attend to that,' the consultant said easily. He opened the door and stood back to let him pass, then stepped forward to smile and beckon to Mary, who had risen from her seat and stood with downcast eyes.

'This way, young lady, if you please.' The voice was bland, impersonal. There was nothing in his manner to indicate surprise at, or disapproval of, anything she had done or might intend to do.

'Your mother is dead. She died two years ago,' her

father whispered, as their paths crossed in the middle of the room.

At least it could never happen again. It had been an unpleasant experience sitting in that waiting room. The woman typing behind the glass had looked right through her with gimlet eyes. She knew. Mary could tell by the way she stared.

It was odd to hear the doctor talk in that everyday voice as he told her all about diseases – things that would have kept her from sleeping for a week if she had let her mind dwell on them, things she had known nothing about at all. She was sick with revulsion when he talked of sores and discharges and the thing going underground for years and breaking out again and becoming incurable.

He told her that she should behave herself and give up 'going' with boys, who would only make use of her and then leave her. He said she should work hard in school and get a job and grow up to be independent. He said that sex was for marriage and one day she would regret it if she didn't change her ways. He was so nice about it that she wondered if she shouldn't tell him everything and ask his advice.

Deep within her she felt disgust for that other one. She wished she'd go away and leave her alone. Everything had become too complicated since her appearance. She wished they'd both go away and there was just her father and herself. She missed her father. If only he came back and was happy, she'd never want anything to do with that pair again.

It was grand to feel the breeze on her burning face as

they went down to the bridge. They had lunch in the
Kentucky: burgers and chips and all the coke she wanted,
ice cream and coffee. He was happy and joking. He said
maybe they should take off to Dublin for a week. He talked
of the time when he was her age and fell in love with some
girl – all about a summer day in the fields. Then she went
away and he never saw her again. He said Mary reminded
him of her.

On the way home he pulled into a lay-by, took out a
packet labelled Durex and wanted to – just like that. Even
the other one was shocked – with the road so near – in
broad daylight – and cars passing.

The doctor's warning and her own guilt made Mary
wonder if she could ever do things like that again. When
she told him she was worried, he was apologetic. He said
she was his love and he'd never do anything to hurt her.
She didn't like it when he talked that way. It was as if he
didn't see her any more, only that other one. He wasn't
interested in being her father.

SEVEN

Day flowed into day like a river that carried him, detached on its broad surface. Cocooned in his own world, he pursued his dream. Once, under cover of a shooting expedition, they had driven up to the hills, where, high in the bracken overlooking the sea and the islands, with a freighter dragging itself like a snail along the horizon, he had pinned a red butterfly slide in her hair and then had taken her. For him it was the perfect recapture – and completion – of his adolescence.

He had barely started when the dry whisper of breeze and bracken was disturbed by another sound. Somewhere to their left came snatches of speech and then the press of feet, crunching and snapping. She had tensed under him in alarm, but he had continued, indifferent to discovery. The day went suddenly dark as she snatched their clothes and pulled them over their heads. The crackling tread came closer and he could distinguish two voices, a boy's and a girl's. 'Jesus!' the girl hissed in a shocked whisper and the footsteps went bursting off in a different direction, until they merged into the bustle and sway of breeze-swept bracken.

Afterwards she had hurried into her clothes and sat at some distance, refusing to look at him. He went across and sat beside her. She removed the slide and handed it silently to him. When he touched her hair in a gesture of reconciliation and tried to put it back, she pulled away.

'It's all right,' he said. 'We were hidden in the bracken.'

'I'm certain that was a girl from school. They could have recognised us.'

'They couldn't. Our heads were covered.'

'They'd know the car down there. They'd guess.'

'Nonsense,' he said. 'We're not the only ones on the mountain today.'

'All the more reason why we should be careful.' Her tone was unforgiving.

'I'm sorry. Things . . . had gone too far.'

He agreed that his behaviour had been reckless. It was a quality that he felt growing in himself, but he seemed helpless to do anything about it. He felt his passion for her expand to absorb all his waking thoughts. The opportunity to satisfy it was limited by the need for secrecy. His love demanded free expression, open acknowledgement, immediate gratification. What it got were furtive and hurried trysts edged with anxiety.

He sat silent at meal times, watching his wife, heedless of the words that came from those pursed, puritanical lips, wondering when the next opportunity would come. The presence of Mary between them, her eyes downcast, her expression one of boredom, gave a fine edge to his impatience. It was a painful pleasure to him to pat her on the arm under those watchful eyes or to touch her hair as they left the table afterwards.

She had enjoyed the drive and the walk up into the hills, the heather wiry and springy underfoot, a view out over the islands and beyond, people like beetles on Kilcummen strand, a cool breeze through brown fern fronds, a sound like the bursting of seed pods all around and grasshoppers everywhere. Butterflies too, big and white, dipping and floating, lighting on top of the bracken with wings raised – from where she was lying, if she squinted hard, they looked like sails far out to sea.

Why did he have to spoil it all, calling for that one there on the open hillside? Even she was frightened. He lost all sense of caution; he was rough and brutal, thinking only of himself. Then when she recognised Kate Linehan, the other one just slipped away, leaving her. Afterwards she sat there and couldn't talk. She couldn't even cry.

The sun still shone; the hillside trembled with summer; all around, larks climbed ladders of air, as they rustled down through the bracken – separately, soberly – silence and shadows between them.

She had become the watcher, lifting the curtain to observe their coming and going, sensing barbs of hostility in their smiles as in their neglect. Sometimes at night they sat and played cards in the kitchen, while she watched television. When the advertisements came up, she would bustle in to busy herself at the sink and listen to their noisy laughter. Without quite knowing why, she would contrive to break up the game, inventing a job for Mary, finding a spent bulb for him to change.

What did she suspect? What was she afraid of? She scarcely knew. What had been done and said while she was away that had polarised everything? Was it just the usual middle-aged crisis that her husband was going through? Was that why he had changed his hairstyle, combing it forward to cover the baldness, and had taken to wearing a ridiculous sailor's cap set at a jaunty angle?

Mary's newfound poise and arrogance seemed to grow out of her relationship with her father. There was a hard edge to her that hadn't been there before, as if she had been sharpened and honed by his indulgence, by his choice of her to replace her mother in the order of precedence in the house. It was clear, at least, that that was what was happening. She was being relegated to an inferior position.

There were other changes that impinged on her consciousness gradually. The house that had once been full of young voices was silent and empty. Neither Angela nor any of Mary's other friends had called since her return from Lourdes. There were no more long telephone conversations, no loitering laughter on the doorstep, no giggling from her bedroom. All her free time was spent with him or scribbling in that diary she kept locked away in a trunk in her room. What was in it that she had to be so secretive about? There was a time – not very long ago – when it was left lying about and had to be constantly tidied away, when it was full of adolescent crises and school gossip. What was she writing in it now? The time might shortly come when it would be a mother's duty to force that lock and find out for herself.

She was still pondering about it as she prepared for her committee meeting. It was the AGM and she would be making her report. The spiritual director would be there. The diocesan co-ordinator might even pay one of his rare visits to commend the work and exhort them to further effort. He might bring with him one of those bright, enthusiastic young men from the mission fields as living proof of their achievement. Somewhere in a folder in her bedroom there were details of all the students they had helped to educate. She must remember to look it up and bring it with her. It would be nice to be able to tell the young man that they remembered him very well, and to give the exact date and place of his ordination. Such attention to detail would be bound to impress the others and pave the way for a second term of office, an honour she would happily have foregone had she not been convinced that someone would have to take the lead in preventing control of the society from falling into the hands of people like Maud, who was too cautious and lacked vision.

Ennis watched her out the door in a mood of impatient elation and saw the last of her from the bedroom window as she turned the corner. He pulled the curtains until they met and the evening light came, mellow and subdued, as into a sunken cave. He summoned Mary and she came reluctantly, as if she were still nursing a grievance. He undressed her slowly, until she stood ready in the middle of her discarded clothes.

He had taken off his own clothes and was carrying her to bed when the door opened and her mother walked in. She stood a moment looking at them, then opened her mouth and screamed – a sound that burst and spurted and gushed and flowed.

'No!' she cried. 'No! No! No!' She hurled herself at him with beating hands, tearing long weals on his naked shoulders with her nails.

He raised his fist and struck her in the face, a violent blow that sent her reeling across the room until she collapsed on the single bed. He locked the door and put the key under his pillow. 'Now you might as well see the rest,' he shouted.

She started to scream again, peal after peal of high-pitched sound. He pulled her into a sitting position and struck her a flurry of blows with his open palm until she subsided into a trembling blubber.

'This is all your doing,' he roared, 'and no one else's.' He sprang to the bed where Mary was crouched, shielding her nakedness with her underclothes. He swept them aside and spread her on her back. 'Look! God damn you, look!' he shouted. He continued to shout as he forced himself on Mary, who cowered under him.

His wife turned away, hid her head in the blankets and covered her ears with closed fists to shut out his yelling climax.

When it was over he collapsed in tears, stroking Mary's terrified body, crying endearments and hoarse apologies. Then he grabbed the key, opened the door and rushed at his wife. He pulled her from the bed and threw her into the corridor so savagely that she struck the wall a jarring blow and slid to the floor. He flung blankets and pillows after her. He wrenched armfuls of clothes from the wardrobe and dumped them on top of her, shouting, 'Get out of my room. Get out of my life. If you ever come in here again, I'll kill you.'

When there was nothing left but a row of shoes, he scooped them up and fired them at her where she cowered on the floor, protecting her head with raised arms. 'They stoned the woman taken in adultery,' he roared. 'It would have matched them better to have spared a few for the wife who refused her husband. That's some kind of crime too, God damn you, and when it comes to the passing of judgement, you'd better remember that.'

He slammed the door and returned to the bed, where Mary lay whimpering. He eased back the blankets and looked into her frightened face. 'I'm sorry,' he said. 'She drove me to it.'

'Why did you have to do . . . that . . . in front of her?'

'You'd have to go back years to find why.' He spoke in a low voice, as if he were talking to himself. 'You put up with something for a long time and then, one day, you can't put up with it any more. I once nearly killed a man. Did I ever tell you about that?' There was no reply and he continued. 'It was in a pub. This fellow kept picking on me. Wouldn't let me alone. I got up and went somewhere else. He followed me. He was very abusive. Spoke in a filthy way about someone I had a high regard for. I warned him. He got more abusive – kept on shouting so that the whole place could hear. Something snapped inside me and I went for him. You can only put up with some things for so long.'

'You shouldn't have done . . . what you did,' Mary said again. 'If she hadn't seen she couldn't be sure.'

'I wanted her to be sure,' he said brutally.

'You weren't thinking of me, then.'

'You're right,' he said, with ready contrition. 'I'm sorry.'

'What are we going to do?' Mary cried.

'I'll tell you what we're going to do. You and I are staying in this room. Bring in your things. She can go wherever she likes.'

'I can't,' she protested.

'You can – and you will.' There was a new harshness in his tone.

'I wish I was dead,' Mary said. 'How am I ever going to face her again?' She covered her head with the blanket and began to cry.

Later, when he got hungry, he went downstairs to forage in the kitchen. He brought her up tea and watched her drink a little in silence.

'Where is she?' Mary asked.

'She must have gone into your brother's old room. There's a light in there.'

'Is she all right?'

'Why wouldn't she be?'

'Don't you think you should go and see?'

'What for?' he said. 'We don't have to care about her.'

'Please,' Mary pleaded.

To humour her he went down the corridor to the bathroom. He stood for a while listening, then closed the door noisily and went back.

'There's nothing wrong with her,' he said in a casual voice.

'What was she doing?'

'What she always does when there's an argument,' he said contemptuously. 'She was down on her knees persuading the Lord that she was in the right.'

When morning came Mary was reluctant to go downstairs. He prepared breakfast and brought it up to her. There was, he assured her, no sign of her mother.

When it was time to open the supermarket, she was still in Tom's room. Around noon Mary came out to the shop to whisper that she hadn't come down yet.

At lunch she still hadn't appeared. Tea time came and went and there was no sign of her. After tea he surprised Mary on the corridor. She was listening outside Tom's door. Seeing him, she went downstairs without a word.

Late at night, when they were in bed, he heard his wife come out and go to the bathroom. Another day came and went and still she did not appear. On the third night he heard her go downstairs to the kitchen. Three further days were to pass before either of them saw her. Sunday had come and gone and, as far as he could ascertain, she hadn't been to mass.

It was midweek before she appeared. One morning he went downstairs and there she was in the kitchen preparing breakfast. She neither looked up nor gave any sign when he came in. She laid his breakfast on the table in front of him in silence. Her face was pale, withdrawn. But there was a determination there, a stubbornness. Obviously she had settled something in her own mind and had come to a decision.

She ignored Mary when she came in. They watched her covertly as she moved about. Her silence was intimidating. For the most part they kept silent too. When they did speak it was guiltily and in whispers. It was as if communication had been proclaimed incestuous as well, and she was daring them to repeat in words the shameless episode of the bedroom.

It was agony to be near them. She couldn't bear to look at

them, much less to speak. The horror of what she had witnessed when she came back to collect the file had struck her dumb. Her fears for Mary were great. She had not gone outside the door since it happened. How could she carry the secret of that crime abroad into the daylight and keep it hidden?

She did her work in the kitchen, cooked whatever was required, washed and ironed and baked, and said nothing. In the evenings, she retreated to Tom's room and sat there, shocked, confused, helpless.

Once, when the two of them had gone out in the car, she slipped into the room and stood staring at the bed. Blankets and sheets were tossed about in disarray. Lying together, in the midst of all the chaos, she saw Mary's pink nightdress and her husband's pyjamas. The obscenity of it drove her in tears from the room.

One evening about two weeks later she dressed for going out and went downstairs. They were in the kitchen, the accounts spread on the table in front of them. They looked up, then studiously returned to their work. Without a word, she let herself out and closed the back door behind her.

In the Square the taxi she had ordered from Fox's garage was waiting. She spoke briefly to the driver, a young man who might have been the same age as her son, and got in. The taxi took her some twenty miles into the country, before turning in at the gates of a demesne with an ornamental arch and a long, winding driveway through wooded parkland. At the end of the drive they came abruptly round a bend to a remarkable building, part medieval manor house, part crenellated castle. The taxi took a wide sweep and deposited her at a massive door, studded with iron bolts. She rang the bell and stood with lowered head. The taxi driver lit a cigarette, picked up the evening paper and settled down to wait.

She heard the door creak open and grate back on dry hinges. The kindly face of a bearded lay brother in grey habit, tied at the waist with a cord, looked down at her. She asked to see one of the monks. No, she didn't know which one. What she required was advice from some priest, wise in the ways of the world and its aberrations. He led her across a huge tiled hall, on which her sharp heels rang, bringing echoes from the vaulted roof, and into a waiting room. No, she would prefer not to give her name. He understood. Secrecy and discretion were hallmarks of the monastery. That was why people came. Father Simon would be able to help her.

When she returned home she went straight to bed. In the morning she was in the kitchen, her manner no longer aggressive. She laid their food in front of them in a quieter, less censorious way. Her behaviour, insofar as it made any statement at all, was neutral, more in the manner of a hired servant resigned to her lot. It wasn't an easy role to play, but she was determined to follow Father Simon's advice. She was not yet ready for conversation, though she knew now that she would have to talk to Mary. If her talk was to do any good, she would have to be circumspect.

When Mary came downstairs in mid-morning, she was ready. The table was set with two cups, a milk jug, sugar bowl and biscuits on a plate. A teapot sat under a blue cosy on the cooker. Mary glanced at the preparations, and thinking that her mother was expecting a visitor, she turned to leave.

'I'd like to speak to you,' her mother said quietly.

She brought the teapot over to the table and began to pour. She pushed a cup towards Mary and pointed to a chair. Mary perched on the edge, poised for flight. Her face was closed and uncompromising. She would listen and that was all. How long she would listen would depend on what her mother had to say.

'I'm not going to give out to you,' she began in a restrained way. 'But I'm very worried about you and' – she hesitated, searching for an inoffensive term – 'what's happening.'

She stopped, waiting for a response. Mary stirred her tea in silence.

'Can't you see that you're the one who's being damaged by all this?' She made as if to stretch her hand across the table and withdrew it again in the face of Mary's cold glance. 'I want you to know that I'm on your side. I want to help you. If he's . . . forcing you, if you're afraid of him, you must tell me. Is he? Please, tell me.'

'You're the only one that's forcing me,' Mary spat.

'What do you mean?' She had the sensation of the ground slipping away under her feet, of chasms opening all round her.

'You were supposed to be his wife,' Mary grated in a cold hard voice. 'But were you?'

Suddenly her temper snapped. With a cry she slapped Mary's face. 'How dare you speak to me like that! How dare you tell me my duty! I forced you, did I? It was me that was responsible for that disgraceful scene in the bedroom, was it? You little fool. Can't you see how he's making use of you, telling you everything was my fault? Is it my fault that he's the sort of father that would seduce his own child?'

'What would you say,' Mary countered with icy passion, 'if I told you it was me that seduced him?'

11 August 1980
Too upset to write anything for ages. She knows everything. The worst, the most awful, the most terrible thing has happened. Can't bear to write about it. Can't bear to think about it but can't think about anything else.

There was a terrible confession that she did not dare to make − even to herself. Somewhere, down under the skin, beyond the blood, part of her had wanted her mother punished like that. She was appalled at the realisation that she could hate her so much. How little, until that moment, she had understood herself and what was hidden inside her. Looking into herself now, she saw horrible things lurking there. She used to think that murderers were a rare, disturbed breed of people and you could go through life without ever meeting one. But now she knew that everyone . . . that she herself . . . God, what kind of person was she anyway?

After the horror, the screaming and the noise, silence − days of it. When her mother didn't appear, she began to wonder if he might have done something worse in a rage. Then she had heard her move about in the darkness and been reassured.

What was to happen next? How did people continue to live together in one house after that? How did they bear to exist in the same world even? What was she to say to her mother the next time they met? What were they to do for the rest of their lives?

She had been appalled at the way he struck her. It was worse – much worse – than having him strike herself. She didn't mind hurting her in other ways, especially in the beginning. Now she didn't know whether she wanted her hurt at all. It wasn't a nice feeling when you wanted people hurt and they actually were hurt. It was a relief when her mother hit her. She could hate her again, and not feel bad about it.

Next time Mary went into the kitchen her mother said she was sorry. It took her by surprise. Her mother had never been one to apologise. She was inclined to prefer her that way. If you knew she was the offender and she wouldn't admit it, you had a reason to resent her. You could feel superior in your mind about it. Apologising upset all the old relationship. It was as if her mother had stolen her right to harbour a grievance.

What she thought about now, as they sat at meal time and said nothing, was how she could escape.

EIGHT

It was mid-August when the young man was hired. It had been Ennis's idea at first, but the business interested him no longer. The conversion of the store had gone ahead under his wife's direction. It was something with which she had become obsessed. He was pretty sure that he understood her motivation in hiring the boy and took sombre satisfaction in obstructing her strategy.

An advertisement had been placed in the *Record*. There were two replies. The first was from a sharp young fellow in the city, who had served his time and was 'looking for a challenge'. He had experience in all departments of hardware. He 'would be tempted by a job which offered responsibility and the opportunity for advancement'. When Ennis had read the letter, which impressed him very much, he tore it up with savage care and threw it into the wastepaper basket.

The second letter, in a childish hand, was from a young improver, serving his time in a local store. There were references from his parish priest and his employer testifying to his honesty and industry. The priest – from a parish ten miles west – spoke well of the boy and his widowed mother.

He liked the look of the fellow when he called for interview. He was shy and awkward – all angles and shiny surfaces. His wrists were long and bony and his trouser ends were climbing up his ankles. His copper hair had an alert, surprised look and his expression was one of painful honesty. His handshake was strong and eager, of the kind that locked and held, until one almost had to remind him that it was time to let go.

Ennis decided at once to hire him. He went through the motions of interviewing him, hardly listening to the answers, and offered him the job. He named a wage that seemed to please the boy, and told him to report for work on the following Monday morning.

His wife, who had been hovering outside in the hope of picking up some of their conversation, was in the hallway when they came out.

'Hugh Dolan from Locknalackann,' he said. 'He's starting on Monday.'

She put out her hand and the earnest young man took it in his strong grip. She eased her fingers free and stood watching as they went down the hallway to the supermarket. From her expression, he could gather that Dolan wasn't exactly the kind of young man she had had in mind.

Mrs Ennis went out of her way to be kind to Dolan, enquiring after the health of his mother and asking if he was comfortable in his digs. It was she who suggested that instead of returning home for lunch he should dine in the house. Lunch hour in the supermarket was irregular, depending on the flow of customers, which in turn depended on the weather and the season. The change would make things easier for his landlady and be more convenient for his employers. A suitable financial arrangement was worked out and from then on he ate in the dining room.

The meal was served by Mary, who padded about never saying a word, except to enquire if everything had been all right. From the kitchen Mrs Ennis could observe that Dolan was as shy as Mary and, apart from thanking her in a whisper, had nothing to say either. For most of the time he kept his eyes downcast, only raising them to watch Mary's back as she withdrew.

It was not a promising beginning but, at least, she had managed to get them together for half an hour every day. Perhaps time would take things further. But she was not hopeful. Dolan was just a raw, self-conscious boy without sophistication or self-assurance. There was little about him to attract a quick, clever girl like Mary. He had neither the looks, manner nor gift of speech to turn a girl's head.

At least he was a man – and a man of very different calibre to the other. But would Mary see that? And would she place any value on it if she did see?

It was clear that Mr Ennis did not approve of the new arrangement. Dolan was aware of that, though he didn't know why. They had discussed it in his presence, Mrs Ennis asserting that it would be more convenient all round, while her husband maintained that it mightn't suit Dolan at all and could cause problems with his landlady.

What puzzled him was a sharpness in their bickering that was out of all proportion to the matter under discussion. His inclination had been to refuse the offer, but he couldn't find the words to decline gracefully. He had no wish to offend either of them, but as Mrs Ennis was the one who would bear the brunt of preparing the meal, he had allowed himself to be carried along on her insistence.

Mary, who served the meal, had a quiet way of coming and going that pleased him. If asked to describe her, he might have said that she was a good-looking girl. If pressed further, he would have admitted that it was pleasant to be served by a shy girl with dark eyes and dark hair. It would be nice if she were to smile occasionally. Perhaps she was too conscious of the difference between them. Perhaps she was too proud to talk to a mere employee.

In the evenings when he wasn't out cycling, or hurling with his friends, he sat in the front room of the terraced house in Mill Street and watched television in the company of Mrs O'Brien, his landlady, a round, motherly soul with grey hair and a warm smile. Her husband, a retired carpenter, sat beside her, his pipe and newspaper at his elbow. He had a workbench in a shed at the back, where there was always a smell of woodshavings and beautifully turned pieces of wood to sniff and handle.

Every day the charade went on. Ennis opened the supermarket, greeted customers and supervised the work. Meals were served and eaten. The accounts were done and bills paid on time.

Everything appeared normal – until bedtime came and they went upstairs, his wife to kneel in desperate prayer in Tom's room, while in the main bedroom he and Mary undressed and went to bed together. When his needs had been satisfied, he liked to lie and talk about their relationship and its effect on their lives. Everything that happened in the house had some bearing on it, or grew directly from it.

Dolan, as a source of contention, was added to the list. His hiring had been controversial. It was recognised by both sides as a tactical gambit in the war between husband and wife, and his presence at the dinner table was bitterly resented by Ennis. In bed he drew his name down casually and listened for nuances in Mary's tone as she responded. She dismissed him in monosyllables. He was 'all right'. He was 'very quiet'. She was aware of his existence – no more.

This was reassuring. On the other hand, girls could be devious. Perhaps her dismissal was too casual altogether. He found himself listening with greater concentration and the beginnings of anxiety to anything she had to say about him, however trivial. She never mentioned Dolan, unless he did first. Was there significance in that? She tended to agree with whatever he said about him. If he criticised him – and his inclination was to criticise more and more – she accepted his criticism. If he had something good to say – a thing he occasionally had, merely as a test – she accepted that too. Was that significant?

He found it equally hard to decide whether Dolan had taken any particular notice of her. When he introduced the subject obliquely by enquiring, 'Well, are they looking after you in there?', as the young man returned from his lunch, Dolan had smiled diffidently and said, 'Yes – fine.' He looked at the clumsily dressed yokel in his cheap suit and thick-soled shoes and hated him for his youth and innocence.

Later he had tried a different approach, asking how he spent his spare time. Dolan confessed that, apart from playing a little hurling in the evenings, he didn't do very much, except walk and read and listen to music. At weekends he went home to visit his mother. As for girls, he blushed and said he didn't know any. Ennis advised him that there was time enough for girls when he had finished his training and made something of himself. He said he disapproved of close friendships between girls and boys of his age, because, too often, they led to unhappiness and heartbreak.

'There's Mary, for example,' he said, judging the moment opportune to sow doubt and confusion. 'You've noticed her a little strange, I suppose?'

'She's very quiet,' Dolan said, after initial hesitation.

'Keeps to herself,' Ennis nodded. 'She's what I'd call a wounded person – hurt in her mind. You won't know this, but some time ago she developed a silly attachment, a schoolgirl crush – call it whatever you like – for an older man. The girls in school knew about it and made her life miserable.'

'That's terrible.' Dolan sympathised in deep embarrassment.

Ennis scrutinised him closely, studying his expression, evaluating the tone of his response, testing it for emotion. 'She moped about the place – stopped going out – wouldn't go to school. The doctor put her on tablets for her nerves. She's been low ever since. So you'll understand why I wouldn't want anybody upsetting her.'

Dolan nodded gravely and said, 'Yes, Mr Ennis.'

'The mind's a slow thing to heal,' he said, and went back to his checking with a satisfied smile on his face.

10 September 1980
Autumn and everyone back at school, everyone except me. I sit here in my old room. It's the only place where I can be free of them and be myself. I sit and think. The blue-grey of the sky is a blind that I pull, shutting everything out. I stare at it until it becomes part of the wall and isn't sky any more, and there's nothing out there, and the world is me and this lined paper and this pen that writes.

She hadn't had nightmares for years. Now she was never free of them. He slept as gently as a baby. She knew now she should never have left her room, should have locked the door and not let that one loose. *She* was the one who unlocked another door and let him in, and since then there had been nothing but disaster. That was why she had to get away from them all.

She didn't mean Hugh Dolan, though. He was as quiet as a speck of dust floating in a shaft of sunlight. He sat there and hardly looked, let alone spoke. He wouldn't like the other one − she was certain of that. She wished she'd go away for good. Maybe that was the way it would end. She kept thinking of it ending. But how? Maybe it would happen naturally, like the leaves falling. She noticed them in the garden, drifting down. She used to think it a sad time of the year. Now it seemed to have some promise of hope.

Her mother had surprised her on the previous afternoon by coming to the door and knocking. She said she wanted to speak to her – speak, not scold. She sat on the bed – very tight in herself. She had been tight too. That was the way her mother affected her. Whatever it was about her mother, she felt the blood rise in herself when she came near. What she meant was that, though her mother was the cause of everything, she always behaved as if she was the injured party.

When her mother said she was worried about pregnancy and the scandal, she told her there was no need, because she had taken precautions. Her mother was as shocked as if she had told her she was three months gone. When she got her breath, she said Mary owed it to herself – and to her father, if she had any regard for him – to stop. She said that if it became known he'd be the one to bear the blame, to go to jail even. She asked if she really wanted that? He had been separated from his better judgement by his unhealthy obsession. There wasn't the same excuse for her.

Her mother wiped her eyes and said she prayed for her every day and that she was not a bad girl – only misled. The other one said it was all a trick to soften her up. But Mary felt sorry for her mother and curious, for the first time, about the kind of person she really was. She could sense that there was somebody there that was, maybe, different from anything she had imagined. The trouble was that she couldn't afford to think about it. It would only have complicated things and, anyway, she was probably wrong.

NINE

When Dolan came to dinner he was mildly surprised to have it served by Mrs Ennis. She looked pale and distraught and laid the meal in front of him with a distracted air. To make conversation he asked about Mary. The question was put tentatively – almost shyly – as if he weren't sure whether he had any right to ask. 'Is your daughter not well today?'

'It's a thing of nothing.' Mrs Ennis brushed the question away with the crumbs she was sweeping from the table. 'She had a little . . . accident.'

'I'm sorry to hear that.'

'Slipped on the stairs.' Her offhand manner made light of the affair. 'She's a nasty black eye. Must have hit the banisters as she fell.'

'I hope she'll be all right soon,' he said.

Everything seemed to be going wrong. There was something inherent in his nature that drove him to excess.

What he had done was unforgivable. The poor girl had been in a state of shock, shivering like a leaf and ice-cold. What lunacy had driven him to strike her? For a devastating moment he had seen that look on her face − hostility, fear, sheer terror − that he had seen before on the face of his wife.

Mary had lain in the room afterwards, her eyes filmed over and frozen, a darkening weal on her cheekbone. He looked down at her, consumed with love and self-loathing. Though he spoke and she listened, he knew there was no communication between them. The shutters were closed over her face and somewhere inside she hid herself from him. He stole into her room several times during the night to look at her. She lay in the subdued light of a bedside lamp, sleepless, inert. When he put a hand on her head, he saw tears brimming in her eyes.

He was up early to bring her tea and fuss about, tidying the bed and smoothing the pillows. Guilt gnawed at him as he looked at the swelling under her eye and the emptiness of her face. On his knees he begged her to forgive him, to say something, to be angry, to shout at him, to hurt him, but not to switch off or ignore him, because he was his own worst enemy to harm the one person he loved.

He took her hand and kissed it, repeating how sorry he was and how ashamed, until she broke into a heave of tears and confused cries. When she grew calm again, he took the sheet and dried her face, then smoothed her dark fringe with his fingers. He swore that he would never again do anything to cause her pain. This was enough to renew her tears. He held her and quietened her with a soft crooning. Later she was persuaded to take a sip of tea. But quickly her expression lapsed into apathy and she withdrew herself from him.

The alert, eager face of Dolan in the supermarket was an affront to him. It was infuriating to have him stop to enquire about Mary's accident.

'Accident?' he said testily. 'What accident?'

'The . . . stairs,' Dolan said deferentially. 'Mrs Ennis was telling me . . . '

'Nothing to trouble yourself about.' Anger choked Ennis at the impertinence of the fellow and the stupidity of his wife in blabbing such things. He nodded in dismissal and watched with a scowl Dolan's receding back. By the very nature of things, he told himself fearfully, it was to some untutored lout like this that he might lose her one day. The young attracted the young. To them inexperience and ignorance were no barrier. They were much more likely to be a bond.

How to shield her from this plague of youth? He could spirit her away. But wherever they went she would take her youth with her. His own rash character, his rages, his fits of violence, would only drive her more quickly in the direction to which youth and inclination drew her. Dolan was not the only threat, but he was the most easily identifiable – and as such he came to hate him.

Ennis was too clever to show his hatred openly. It was something that he warmed in the secrecy of his mind. Like a carefully tended reactor, it never quite went critical, but there were minor flares, scurries and alarms. He gave vent to his feelings by disparaging Dolan to shoppers. He caused confusion in the hardware section, removing or hiding items and then embarrassing the fool by exposing the mess in a pained way in the presence of customers.

On impulse, now, he followed him down through the

densely packed shelves. 'By the way,' he lassoed him with his casually querulous tone, 'I had a woman in complaining . . . ' He paused, noting the shiny lapels, the thrusting Adam's apple that pressed the skin of his throat white, the few sandy hairs that the inexpertly handled razor had missed.

'Something wrong?'

He savoured Dolan's anxiety. 'I told her there must be some mistake. She said there was no mistake. She'd ordered the thing from you ages ago.'

'What did she order?' He was upset, his pride in himself undermined.

'Some kitchen gadget. What difference does it make? She won't be back.'

'I'm sorry.' Dolan scratched his head, disconcerted, caught off balance.

Ennis watched in grim amusement as he backed and stumbled away.

15 September 1980
Whatever I do – bathe it in cold water, hold lumps of ice to it – I'm going to have a black eye. My mouth is cut at the corner and is very sore. All because I went to bed in my own room when my period came.

He had said he was sorry afterwards – he was always sorry afterwards – but she should have told him. He apologised and said he'd lost his head and gone wild because of the locked door.

She was terrified when he broke in and dragged her out by the hair and punched her about the face. Her mother made it worse by trying to stop him. She threatened to go for the guards and the priest and tell them everything. He pushed her from him and the crack that her head made against the wall sounded as if her skull was split. She rolled down the stairs and lay on the first landing without a stir. But she must have recovered, because by the time he had dragged Mary screaming into the bedroom and locked the door and thrown her on the bed, she could hear her twisting the knob and shouting at him to let the child go.

All the time he was at it her mother shook the door and called on God to strike him dead in his sins.

When he had finished, he was covered in blood. Her legs were bloody, too, and the sheets had red patches that went dark in the middle. He opened the door and looked down at his wife where she crouched against the wall. He spat on her in contempt, and came back into the room.

He had been different then, his rage gone, crying that he loved her and had nobody in the world only her. But she could not respond to him or to anything he said. It was as if she had no feeling and no emotion left in her at all, only a great tiredness and a crushing weight of hopelessness.

When he went downstairs she crept to her own room. Her mother came in and found her pale and shivering. She brought in a damp sponge from the bathroom and bathed her eye. Hearing him come up the stairs again, she retreated to Tom's room and locked the door.

Her mother and herself seemed to have exchanged roles. He was beginning to treat her as he was used to treating his wife. How difficult it was for her to acknowledge that. She felt sad and low. She hated her body and herself.

*   *   *

He knocked on the door of Mary's room before entering. Her eyes followed him warily. The swelling, he saw, had subsided but her cheekbone was ribbed with purple that shaded off to puce around the eye itself.

'I got you a present.' He held it out to her with shame-faced diffidence.

She took the package without enthusiasm and laid it on the bedside chair.

'I'd like you to open it.' His tone was submissive, pleading. He hung over her anxiously, rubbing his fist inside his palm and shifting from foot to foot.

'What is it?' she asked, in a voice that held too little curiosity for his liking – and no excitement or pleasurable expectation at all.

'Open it and see.'

She picked up the package and began to unwrap it. What he wanted to see more than anything was life come back into that sad face and light glitter in her cheerless eyes. It was almost a week since their quarrel and he was anxious for reconciliation.

She dropped the wrapping paper and stared at the expensive-looking box covered in dark blue velvet. She lifted the lid which snapped back on hinges and locked. Inside was a watch with oval face and gold bracelet.

'Well, do you like it?' He searched her face for signs of animation and was dismayed when he saw a tear form in her eye and swell and tremble.

'What's the matter? What's wrong?'

She wiped her eye and blew her nose and said nothing.

'Don't you like it?'

'Yes.'

'Why the tears, then?'

'It's the way you . . . frighten me.' She faltered.

'I'm sorry. It's that damn black side of me that comes on like a thunderclap and the harm's done before I can stop it. I'd go on my knees a thousand times a day if it would only make things better between us. Tell me you'll forget that it ever happened.'

'If you don't frighten me again − or hurt . . . her,' she whispered.

'I give you my solemn word.' He took the watch from the case. 'Here, let me put it on. If it's too big, or you don't like it, or you'd prefer something else, I can always change it.'

'It's . . . fine,' she said without enthusiasm.

'Maybe you and I should go off somewhere for a holi-day, when . . . you're all right again. This place − being cooped up all the time − it's a strain, isn't it? Don't you feel it a strain? It has a bad effect on me. It makes me tense. It makes me do things I had no intention of doing. It's the atmosphere − her trying to come between us − that fellow watching all the time, his eyes following you around. Did you ever feel it? Well, I do. What do you say? Just you and me − to make up for' − he gestured helplessly − 'all this?'

'I − I don't know.'

'Think about it.' He looked at her anxiously. 'You are feeling better . . . about . . . everything . . . now, aren't you?'

'I'm all right,' she said, but her face had not yet acquired the trick of harmonising with her voice. It remained sub-dued, almost expressionless.

At night as he lay alone there was plenty of time to wonder whether it was, or ever would be, all right again. Would she ever come back to him as trusting and simple as before? Would she ever come back to him at all? Unless she came willingly, there was no comfort in it. What joy could there be in a forced return?

Mrs Ennis sat on Tom's bed in defeat. She had gone into Mary's room and found it empty. The desecration of her house was to continue. She looked around at the mementoes of her son. That picture of him, looking angelic in surplice and soutane, was taken when he was ten. What a devout altar boy he had been. Tears came as she considered his subsequent development. Ten was the ideal age for a boy. He was at his loving and innocent best then. Everything afterwards – though there were flashes of beauty – was anti-climax. A picture of him in school sports gear, his right foot resting on a football, showed him already coarsening into difficult adolescence.

By morning she had steeled herself to be in the kitchen when they came down. The window was open to let in the thinning September sunshine and the radio was playing. She watched them covertly as she prepared the meal. There was only a faint hint of discoloration now around Mary's eye. She watched the way their hands met over the plate and she knew that the disgusting link that bound them had been reforged.

As she sat down to her own meal the sunshine went sour on her. She left the table and rushed upstairs to lock herself in the bathroom. How was she to carry through this charade? How was she to go on pretending? Wasn't it her duty to speak out and to continue to speak until Mary listened?

When she came down again, Mary was sweeping the

kitchen. She closed the door and stood with her back to it, determined to have her say.

'Your eye is much better,' she began in a conversational tone.

'Yes.' Mary made as if to go out, and finding her way barred, retreated to the table. Something about her defiant stand annoyed her mother.

'How long do you think it will be until it happens again?' Her voice was hard, the friendliness of her opening observation gone. 'It will happen again, you know, and the next time it may be worse.'

'There won't be any next time. He promised.'

'Promised!' her mother said scornfully. 'I know all about his promises. For God's sake, girl, will you have sense. That man'll promise anything to get what he wants – and when he's got it, it's goodbye promises!'

'I want to go now,' Mary said.

'Did you ever think where all this is leading you?' Her mother stood firm, her hands behind her holding the door knob. 'It's cutting you off from people of your own age.'

'What harm!' Mary shot back in that maddening way of hers.

'What about Angela and Triona? Why do they never come here any more? It was grand when you were all sitting around that table there, drinking tea and talking about school and laughing and being like young girls should.'

'Fuck Angela and Triona – and you too!' Mary shouted. 'I want out.'

The deliberate coarseness struck Mrs Ennis like a blow. She felt the blood rise in her. It would be so easy to say something that would end the conversation. But it would only mean that she would have to start again at some future time – and she would be starting from a lower base. Her hands whitened on the knob as she fought to control herself.

'Have you ever thought what Tom would say about all this?'

'Tom would be a great one to say anything. Tom of all people!'

They had never been close. She should have remembered that. Tom was almost four years older than Mary. He had been little more than a face opposite her at the table, part of her daily landscape, but a cipher as far as feeling or understanding had been concerned.

'He's your brother. He's a right to know what's going on in his own family.'

'What does his family know about him? He could be dead for all we know.'

'Don't say that!' her mother cried. Mary had put into brutal words the kind of things she herself had been shying away from in the sleepless nights, as she lay in his room, in his bed. Fear of disaster had been linked in her mind, for a long time now, with thoughts of Tom.

'Leave him out of this, then,' Mary warned.

Mrs Ennis relaxed her grip on the door knob. She was aware of the same claustrophobic unease in her daughter's presence as she had felt so many times before. Neither of them, she knew, liked to be alone together. They had little in common, little to talk about. The profundity and range of their silence communicated their mutual antagonism.

The idea came to her that, perhaps, she was wronging the girl. Could it be that what Mary felt was not hatred at all but indifference, an imperviousness that left her invulnerable? Was it indifference or hatred that had led her to supplant her mother?

'Is it because you're afraid? Is that why you do it?'

'No,' Mary said defiantly.

'Why, then?' her mother said. 'I don't understand you at all.'

'You never did.' It was a statement, a boast, maybe, but not a criticism. There was something perverse in the girl that rejoiced in misunderstanding.

'Tell me, then. Why did you do it? Why did you go back?'

'It's something you'd never understand.'

'Tell me,' her mother shouted.

'All right, then!' Mary said. 'I'll tell you. Somebody must act the woman in this house. He's a right to that much, at least.'

Dolan was pleased to find that Mary was serving lunch again – even if it was with her usual abstracted air. He noticed that, apart from a slight discoloration, her eye showed no sign of bruising. When she brought out a bowl of soup on a wooden tray and laid it in front of him, he thanked her. As she turned to leave he coughed and spoke again.

'Have you . . . recovered from your fall?'

She blushed in confusion and put her hand to her cheek.

'Your eye,' he prompted. 'Is it all right again?'

'Yes,' she said and withdrew.

Making conversation with her was as painful as chewing nails. Yet there was something about her that drew him. She looked lost, and so very vulnerable.

When she came out to remove his soup bowl and serve

the main course, he had fallen back again on his usual 'thank you'.

'Was it . . . all right?' he heard her ask.

'Fine,' he said. 'It was fine.' Then, to keep silence at bay and prop up the conversation a little longer, he added, 'Just fine.'

She went away a little less precipitately and it seemed to him that progress had been made.

'It's nice out today,' he said when she came back with his pudding.

'Yes. Very sunny for September.'

She looked, he thought, a little wistful, a little sad. Perhaps it was her mood, or perhaps it was the time of year. September was full of sober melancholy. 'The leaves will soon be away,' he said.

'Yes,' she agreed.

'Still, they give a bit of colour when they're going.' He tried to bring back a little cheer into the conversation, which already was something of a miracle.

'Yes . . . nice reds and yellows.'

'I was at home for the weekend,' he told her. 'The woods were a marvel.'

'Do you come from the country?' she asked diffidently.

'Yes, I go home almost every weekend to see my mother. She lives on her own, you know.'

Silence again while she retreated to the kitchen to fetch his coffee.

He sensed that her difficulty with conversation had nothing to do with her attitude to himself. It was more as if she had grown out of the way of talking to others. Maybe it was the result of her unhappy experience.

'Do you like the country?' he asked when she came

out again.

'Yes, but I don't know very much about the land or the animals.'

'You could learn,' he said, then changed the subject abruptly. 'Was it very sore – the eye?'

'It was stupid – banging into the door like that,' she said uneasily.

He remembered her mother's version of the accident and tried to square it with Mary's. Why should there be contradictory versions? And why should her father have been so short with him when he had mentioned it?

That reserved look had come over Mary's face again. She left the room and did not come back.

At lunch time the following day it seemed to him that she entered the room with less reluctance and left with less alacrity. She even managed a smile. Her face, he noted, was pale.

What she needed was to get out into the country and let the autumn breeze whip some colour into her cheeks and sweeten those parts of her mind that had gone morose. He thought it might be pleasant to walk with her through the woods of Barton's demesne on Sunday afternoons. They could wander together down some shady vista towards the distant voice of water and descend to where the Coorbane river went belling over the weir into a dark pool.

He noticed that she dressed in a dowdy way. Her denim skirt hung crookedly. She wore neither ear-rings nor a bracelet nor any jewellery, apart from an expensive-looking watch. She didn't wear lipstick or paint her nails. Why was she content to remain at home like that, when others her age were either at school or out in jobs?

He was still wondering about it when the door burst

open and her father, cross and impatient, blustered in to tell him that he was needed urgently in the supermarket.

Mary sat in her room and wondered why she had gone back. She didn't know. It was partly for the sake of peace, partly because she felt marked by him, soiled by him – his property – partly because she knew that, sooner or later, he would come for her again.

It had been wrong to say such things to her mother, but that was the effect she always had on her. She made you want to hurt her. The sad thing was, that part of what she said was true. Only for her, that wild one would never have appeared.

Hugh Dolan wouldn't like that one. How could he? She was disgusting. He had talked about his own place. He'd be different in those woods, more himself, more assured. Everybody had some place where they were more themselves than anywhere else. She wondered where her place was. She thought it would be very simple and very plain, with nothing complicated in it. It would be completely ordinary and nothing unusual would ever happen there.

She could never let Hugh know anything about that one. The nice thing was that, when he was about, she wasn't there. That was what she liked about him. She felt drawn to those woods. It would be nice to walk there, to talk and have nothing on her mind at all.

TEN

Sometimes while she slept beside him he lay awake and thought of the past. All his life had been an effort to re-create that past or, at least, one little part of it. It was possible now to believe that he had achieved his dream. But how to preserve it, how to protect it?

Sexually he had been a precocious boy, coming to puberty and an awareness of his own body early. It had begun with a restlessness, a need to get out of the house, to exercise himself, to be doing things. Then it would manifest itself in a lethargy, an inclination to lie about and let his mind wander. More and more, he found it wandering among bare limbs – glimpses of girls on passing bicycles and bathers on the strand. More and more, he set out to contrive such encounters.

Of girls he knew little, until one summer's afternoon his restlessness took him walking through the fields, stripped to the waist, his shirt thrown carelessly over his shoulder. He was just thinking how pleasant it would be to find a sheltered bank and lie there, when he leaped over a ditch and there she was, stretched out on the grass, her limbs spread and her skirt pulled high – a bright, shining girl, who gave a start and then smiled at him.

He hesitated, tongue-tied. She stared back at him with a grin, her black hair curling over her eyes, and made no attempt to correct the disarray of her dress. They spent a long minute there, looking in silence. She was not anyone he knew, though her face was familiar and he thought she came from the other side of town.

He turned to go.

'What's your hurry?' she called.

'No hurry at all.'

'Sit down, then' – she smoothed the grass – 'till I show you something.'

He sat down near her. She drew closer until they were almost touching. He could get the warm smell of her body, mixed with the scent of crushed grass and a woodbine tang that might have come from the hedge behind. She was about a year older than him – perhaps sixteen or a little more. She was smiling – maybe laughing – at him.

'Would you like to kiss me?'

He smiled shyly, but made no attempt to kiss her.

'Don't you want to?' she teased. 'I thought all boys wanted to.'

He nodded, but still hesitated.

'I'll kiss you, then.' She leaned over and swiftly brushed his mouth with hers, then drew back. 'You may go now, if you like. Do you want to?'

He shook his head.

'Boys never do – after that,' she laughed. 'It's very hot. I think I'll take off my blouse. Would you like me to?'

'If you want to,' he answered diffidently. She had a red

cotton blouse on, buttoned down the front.

'Would *you* like?'

He nodded and she laughed. 'Boys are all the same,' she said, unbuttoning her blouse in a lazy way.

He stretched back so that he could watch her guardedly. She had nothing on underneath. He saw her back, white and smooth against her black hair. He saw the curve of her spine and the silky movement of her shoulder blades under the skin as she removed her arms from the sleeves. She tossed the blouse away carelessly and lay back beside him.

Casually she turned on her side to look at him. 'Well?' she challenged. 'You never saw a girl like that before, did you?'

'No,' he admitted, his eyes staring.

She rolled over until one breast rested on his hand. 'You can touch me if you like.'

He held the nipple lightly between finger and thumb. She wriggled in delight. 'That's lovely,' she sighed.

She reached forward and pulled his head towards her and kissed him hard. He let his hands roam over her, feeling her ribs under the surface, dipping into the hollow of her belly.

Suddenly she pushed him away and sat up. 'Don't run before you can walk,' she laughed. 'There'll be time for that – later.'

A muffled soughing outside the room disturbed his thoughts, a sound as light as the fall of leaves on grass. He lay alert in the darkness, listening to the listener on the other side of the door, until, with a sigh like the passing of a ghost, she drifted off.

She had been a handsome girl in those days, reared by

aunts when her mother had died in childbirth – an only child, wilful and pampered. He had delivered groceries to the house on Saturday afternoons. She had answered the door one treacherously sunny day – a fair girl with bobbed hair tied with blue ribbon, a forthright, superior girl, who looked at him directly and found him wanting. He was a servant, delivering groceries, and he should have knocked on the kitchen door. On his way out she had been lying in wait for him.

'Hey, you!' she had called. 'Can you mend a tennis racquet?'

'No, I can't,' he had shouted, 'and even if I could, I wouldn't.'

He had cycled off whistling.

The next time she had been a little more friendly, merely observing with a hint of admiration, 'You're a cheeky fellow, aren't you?'

26 September 1980
Angela came to the door today – the first time for months. She let her in. Heard her voice in the hall, its over-friendly tone. Felt like hiding.

Why did she have to overdo it? '*Angela*, come in, come in. We haven't seen you for ages. Mary was just talking about you. You were always such great friends. She'll be *delighted*.' Maybe she had sent for Angela in the hope of using her influence. That was the first thing you thought about, when she put on that tone – insincerity, pretence, a sort of gushing that made a person cringe. 'Mary! Mary!' – her voice almost hysterical – 'Guess who's here!' She had decided to stand her ground. She wasn't afraid of Angela. They used to be best friends. The difference now was that Angela hadn't grown up.

The talk had been all about school and what the girls said and did, and, when her mother (so tactful of her) went out to leave them together, about Mr Hurley who had been nice to her . . . a lifetime ago.

'What happened your eye?' Angela asked. 'Had a row with your fellow?' She laughed in that empty way of hers. It was clear that she didn't expect an answer. All she wanted was to make a joke and go on to show how exciting and interesting her own life was compared to hers.

'Bumped into something,' Mary said vaguely.

But Angela was already talking about some new boy who had come to town – tall, dark eyes, very intense. His father worked in the Allied Irish and drove a silver – you know – one of those German thingies. She'd played mixed doubles with him on the tennis court – smashing backhand – posh boarding school – Glen-something – she'd think of it in a minute. All the girls drooling. That silly Nuala thing – the one with the glasses and the brace – following him around, making a laughing stock of herself. The cheek of her . . .

Her mother came back and made tea and gossiped away as if she was a girl herself. Angela and she had a great time. They were still at it. If she left the door ajar, she could hear them.

No, she wasn't going out with Angela. No, she didn't want her to come again. She had no intention of visiting her house or going to those boring youth club discos. They were all a clique there, and if you didn't belong, you didn't belong.

She'd outgrown Angela – who professed to know everything and really knew nothing. What would she say if she heard about the other one? She could never tell her. They used tell each other everything. Now she felt an old woman, while Angela . . . Maybe, in twenty-five years' time, they'd be friends again, but she doubted it.

Angela had said she was going to become a teacher. It was all so predictable. She'd come back to the convent and carry on the old tradition – all that nonsense they used to rebel against and say they'd love to springclean out of the way like so much rubbish. She'd tell the pupils her school days were the best days of her life and, what was more, she'd believe it. She'd marry some fellow like that Allied Irish paragon and, maybe, wake up some day when he ran away with some fancy woman and left her with half a dozen kids to look after. That'd be the day Angela grew up, but she couldn't wait till then for her, could she? It was goodbye Angela.

Mary wondered why – if she despised her so much – she felt weepy for Angela?

Hugh valued his visits to the dining room. It was a calm interlude in a busy day, followed by evenings that were lonely. Loneliness was something new for him. One day, it wasn't there, and the next, he was struck down.

The dining room was a quiet place, quietly furnished. There was a round mahogany table with six chairs and a sideboard, also of mahogany, and a clock with weights and pendulum that filled the room with its slow, grave ticking. When it struck, the sound, deep and resonant, hung and trembled, until it faded into the furniture, giving it a darker, mellower sheen.

The day was noteworthy, because it was the first time in his recollection that Mary had set out to cultivate conversation.

'How is business today?' she asked, as soon as he came in.

'Good,' he said, and lapsed into silence, unequal to the demands that the new situation made on him.

'Are you going home for the weekend?'

'Yes,' he said, wondering how the exchange might be kept alive.

'To walk in the woods?'

'Yes,' he said again. 'Do you get out to the country at all?'

'Sometimes.' Her face darkened as if she were avoiding an unpleasant memory. 'I usually go to the sea. But it's late in the year for that now.'

'Unless you like walking on the strand.'

'Do you enjoy that?' she asked.

'A few of us play hurling there on a fine evening if the tide is out. Sometimes we go fishing in an old boat for pollack or mackerel.'

The conversation continued during the meal. By the coffee stage he was courageous enough to ask, 'Do you ever go to discos or go dancing at all?'

She shook her head and did not answer. He saw tears glisten in her eyes. She busied herself about the table, gathering dishes and brushing crumbs onto a plate. She sniffed as she did it. He wondered what he had said that could have distressed her.

She gave a little cough as she was about to leave. 'I used to go to discos quite a lot – but not any more.'

He resisted the temptation to ask why, lest it upset her again. 'Maybe you'd change your mind about that. Maybe you'd come with me, sometime?'

She left the room quickly and in the silence that followed he heard her sobbing in the kitchen.

The following day when he went into lunch her mother served the meal. He had never been sure about Mrs Ennis. She seemed a distant kind of woman, who rarely smiled and then only in a momentary fashion like a lighthouse flash. The smile began with her teeth and ended there. Behind was the impression of great coldness. To be fair, however, she had never been unkind to him – rather the reverse.

He wondered about Mary and why Mrs Ennis was eyeing him in that way of hers. She looked as if she had something to say, but didn't know how to begin. To break a silence that was becoming embarrassing, he asked if Mary was well.

'She's fine,' Mrs Ennis assured him. 'By the way, I couldn't help hearing what you said to her yesterday.'

'I'm sorry if I said anything out of the way . . . ' he began.

'You asked her to go to a disco . . . ' The tone – whatever it was – didn't seem to be disapproving.

'Yes, I did. I'm sorry if you think I shouldn't have.'

'It's nothing like that. It's just that she hasn't been well lately.'

'Mr Ennis mentioned something about that,' he said.

'I think it might be a good thing for her to get out and meet people of her own age,' she said, wondering just what it was her husband had told him. 'The problem is that her father doesn't agree.'

'I knew he was worried about her,' he said. 'I shouldn't have asked.'

'You had every right to ask. It upset her because she couldn't go. Maybe you'd ask again, when her father's away. He's sometimes away on business.'

'But he wouldn't like that, would he?'

'What he doesn't know won't hurt him,' she said.

What date was it? What did it matter? Every day was the same as every other. Sweeps of rain on the window. Trees in the garden like moulting hens huddled against the weather. There was no one to talk to, no one to confide in. It would soon be lunch time in school. Table tennis – hot soup or tea – girls standing around gossiping. She hated her life now. She should never have started. She just wanted to be herself and not be owned by anyone.

I'd like to make this plain: I'm not that one. I don't want to be like her. I don't want to be mistaken for her. More and more, she goes off and leaves me to take her place. He wants her and when he finds she's not there I'm the one to suffer. Would love to go back to my cosy little room and be myself. I could read or do whatever I liked. I could turn off the light and go to sleep and know I'd be safe till morning.

When he came looking she was so terrified that she couldn't respond or do any of the things she was expected to do. She just lay there and cried, without making a sound, because, if she did, he'd be angry. That was something new she had learned – how to cry without attracting attention. Afterwards she turned away and lay there, feeling cold and wakeful, and thought of the next day and the next and the next, and the tears, like rain on the window, washing her face.

It was nice of Hugh to ask. What would he say if he knew? If she herself was disgusted – horrified – what would he feel? She'd never been out – never would now – with any boy. What must he have thought of her? Better whatever it was, than if he'd known the truth. She was so ashamed. She could never look any decent boy in the eye again. If only he had come earlier.

There was no one to talk to, no one to ask for help. Her mother wouldn't understand. She was part of the problem. Why shouldn't she run like Tom? She could pack her things, take some money and go to Dublin. She could get a job and leave them to work it out whatever way they liked. It was their responsibility – not hers.

But it wasn't so simple, was it? It had happened. It couldn't be undone. She was the kind she was now, and even if nobody else knew, she knew and that made all the difference. She hated herself. What wouldn't she give to be back in the spring – to be Angela or Triona. She thought of them in school together, cosy in their own little world, cut off from the outside. She wouldn't fit in with school any more. She was the outside, now.

ELEVEN

He had been a strange, impassioned creature from the start. She remembered how, shortly after their honeymoon, he had brought her out to a field overlooking the town and urged her to join him in cavorting about, mother-naked, in the summer grass. She hadn't done it, though she had stripped down to her bra and skirt just to please him, because she had wanted to please him in those days. She had allowed him to put a hair slide with a red butterfly in her hair. Then, like a shameless savage, he had taken off everything, and while she stood on the ditch, looking about in embarrassment, he had cartwheeled around, whooping and working himself up into a frenzy.

He had pleaded with her to come down and make love to him in the grass. He had stood, looking up, flushed, tumescent, revolting – a predatory smile on his wet mouth.

'No,' she had said. 'Whatever we are, we're not animals.'

He had wheedled and begged, and when she had

promised that, if he put on his clothes, they could go home and – even though it was the afternoon and not the time for such things – he could take her to bed and have his way with her, what thanks had she got? He had, unaccountably, turned away and collapsed on the grass and given himself up to a most unmanly sobbing.

How could anyone cope with a husband like that? Such behaviour was not rational. There was a deep well of emotion in him, as treacherous as a quagmire in the middle of firm ground, and as hard to find or fathom.

When she thought of that first night, she turned instinctively away. It had been such a shock, such a humiliation. No one had ever told her what to expect. Her aunts had given her the usual veiled warnings and the injunction that good Catholic girls never refused their husbands, whatever the circumstances, whatever their private feelings might be. She remembered the hotel bedroom with the high, white ceiling. It was still only dusk when he had steered her up the stairs, with the eyes, as she felt, of everyone in the lobby on them, and locked the bedroom door behind them. She remembered the sound of that key very well. It was inextricably entwined in her mind now with the concept of marriage.

Disrobing had been an awkward, shy affair on both sides. In bed he had begun by touching her feet tentatively with his. Even this she had found alarming. What happened afterwards was like a nightmare. She could endure the clumsy kisses, the awkward fingers that pinched where they meant to caress, the painful fumbling between her thighs. But when, mumbling and hoarse, he had sought her co-operation in stimulating himself, when he found her hands and steered them towards his body, she recoiled in horror and turned away, sobbing. What was it about men that made them so bestial, so depraved, so corrupt in their desires?

Later, after long silences, with apologies and tears on both sides, it had begun again. She had endured the handling and the rough endearments, had tried to make herself responsive, but when he attempted to enter her, she had tightened in terror and held herself rigid. So it had gone on, while the hotel noises and the street noises faded and the light went and the room was swallowed in blackness and the only sound was their heavy breathing. They dozed and fumbled and drew away, until, imperceptibly, the darkness began to lighten again and the bed was revealed with crumpled blankets and sheets, and sprawled limbs touched naturally at last as they lay spread in exhaustion, his hand thrown carelessly across her back.

She awoke to feel his fingers on her and tried to move away. She saw his face close to hers as he struggled to kiss her. She saw it grow red and twist in anger.

'I'm your husband,' he shouted.

She fought back in a panic, and as he pressed his mouth to hers, she bit wildly and deep. Blood burst from his lower lip and she felt it drop on her face. He cried out in pain, then drew his fist and struck her in the mouth. She felt herself grow faint and saw him looming above her; she felt his brute weight on her, pushing her legs apart. She lay whimpering under him, nursing her suffering to feed the great anger that she felt building up in her against him. When he had finished she lay there, sobbing quietly.

He had been immediately contrite and pleaded to be forgiven, touching her in a placatory way. It seemed to her that she had not known him at all, that she was married –

bound for life – to a violent stranger, who could lose his temper and go berserk and do disgusting things in pursuit of animal satisfaction. How did she know that he didn't want it again straightaway and these overtures were nothing more than the first impulse towards a new assault? If it was so, she would be prepared. She would not fight him. She would submit. But every time, she would despise him a little more. Every time, she would console herself with the thought of how much more fine and decent women were than men, how much more in control of themselves, how much more of the spirit burned in them, how much less of the beast.

The second time, as if to confound her, he had been gentle and loving and willing to forego his own gratification when she had been seized with a fit of trembling. He had hushed her and called her his love and swore he would never touch her again except when she wanted him to and that it was happiness enough for him to have her near and be allowed to look after her.

He had taken her sightseeing and brought her out for rows on the lake and gathered a posy of flowers for her and never once sought to kiss her or lay a hand on her for two whole days, content to wait until she was ready. She knew she never would be ready. But she was young and life ran strongly enough in her, and the sunshine and the unaccustomed attention pleased her so greatly that she was surprised at how much she was enjoying herself.

It was only when night came and the question of the shared bed loomed large that she felt apprehensive. She began to develop a headache about twilight and went to bed early. Sometimes she was asleep before he came up. If she were awake, the headache was usually so severe that he had to press wet towels to her forehead and comfort her until she dropped off to sleep. Sometimes she awoke to feel his fingers creeping like mice across her breasts, but at the least shudder or change of breathing on her part, he turned noisily away and left her alone.

Eventually, because she was a good Catholic and because a priest in confession had told her she must, she had allowed him to try again – making it clear that it must be without frills or preliminaries. She undertook to do nothing that might frustrate his intentions, as long as those intentions were honourable, as long as the matter was not spoken about beforehand or analysed afterwards, as long as he kept silent while the deed was taking place, required no participation on her part, made no physical contact with her except under cover of sheets and darkness.

The whole sorry business was to be reserved for the secrecy of the bedroom, with suitably decent intervals of abstinence, which were never clearly defined. Once a week might be reasonable, her confessor was inclined to think, with a complete ban on intimacy as soon as she became pregnant. Intercourse was for procreation – not for self-indulgence. It was a lamentable way to ensure the survival of the race, but as it was God's plan, one was not free to criticise it. On the other hand, there was no compulsion to be enthusiastic about it.

Occasionally in his love-making he brushed over a little exuberance of flesh, which she had noticed and worried about as an adolescent. The touch had a pleasant and strange effect on her. Whenever, in his ignorant striving, he touched that secret place, something in her leaped and just as quickly died, and the act of love became for her a deep source, not just of shame and degradation, but of melancholy, of gloom, of a sense of deprivation, of being alone, without sympathy or understanding.

She had longed to become pregnant so that the thing might stop. When she had, he took to going out at night, returning in a confused, carping state. She had been too absorbed in the novelty of her condition to be more than mildly irritated by his absence. As long as he kept to his own side of the bed, she could tolerate his drunken ways. Inevitably the time had come when he had breached that line.

'We'll have a dare,' the girl said and ran her tongue teasingly around her lips. 'I dare you to take off all your clothes. If you do, so will I.'

When they were naked they looked at each other and laughed a vigorous, pagan laugh, as if the spirit of Pan was abroad in the fields. Neither spoke, but together they raced about in circles, shouting and hallooing, rolling in the grass, throwing tufts of it at each other, chasing and being chased, pulling each other down in a tangle of limbs, enjoying the sun, their nakedness, their youth. Eventually they came to rest, breathless and flushed.

It was natural for him, then, to slide his hands over her body, and it was natural for her to touch him curiously, until his body tensed and spurted seed that shone like spume in the sunlight. As she looked in surprise he kissed her violently. Then he threw himself back, his body and eyes heavy and drowsy.

He yawned and felt himself sink away into a warm sleep, in which he roamed along a sunlit strand, with white waves breaking in drifts of cheesecloth, that fell and spread and floated towards him on an underflow of green.

If it wasn't right, he got mad and told her she was no better than you-know-who and had no warmth and nothing to give. He said they were all the same and there never was a woman yet – except one (whoever she was) – who could satisfy all the needs of a man. It seemed to Mary that the opposite was equally true: many women would be satisfied to be left alone, and she didn't know whether that was a thing he – or any man – was capable of doing for a woman.

She now began to think there might be two sides to the story – her mother's as well as his. How did she know that the version she always thought was true, really was true? Whose word had she for it? Whose word could she trust any more? She could only trust her experience, and it told her that her mother wasn't always to blame.

Hugh was a centre of calm in that mad house. He came, he did his work, he went. He smiled because he was happy. The surface of him was the heart of him. She kept wondering how he would react if he knew. She had started to write him a letter once – she knew she'd never finish it, let alone give it to him – to try and explain how it had come about and how, maybe, it mightn't be as wicked as a person might imagine. She wanted someone to understand that though she knew the thing was monstrous she didn't feel a monster at the time. She hadn't done it because she wanted to defy any law, or to offend God. She had done it to help him. She had done it because she loved him. She still loved him, in spite of everything, but that didn't stop her from being afraid of him.

She knew, too, that understanding her mother a little better and realising that she might be the injured party didn't – and couldn't – make her love her, although she would have liked to. Love or hate didn't come by order.

Sometimes she thought she was all hate and the only thing she could say by way of excuse for herself was that she wished the hate was out. But she didn't know how to get rid of it. Maybe she couldn't get rid of it, without getting rid of herself. Maybe it was herself. Maybe. Maybe God would be good to her, some day, and strike her dead.

Coming down the corridor, he heard talk in the dining room. He opened the door noisily and looked in. Both of them were sitting at the table, their heads supported by their hands and foolish smiles on their faces. Mary sprang up with an expression of guilt and went out meekly, head down. He closed the door after her and turned angrily to Dolan.

'I want a word with you.'

'Is there something wrong?' Hugh asked deferentially.

'You were hired to work out there – not to waste time gossiping here.'

Hugh looked at his watch. 'I'm not due back until half past.'

'Who said you were entitled to spend your whole dinner hour in here?'

'I was just finishing,' Hugh protested.

'I told you that girl was to be left alone. If you can't have your dinner without troubling her, you'd better make other arrangements.'

'We were only talking.' Hugh leaped up.

'Look here,' Ennis said in a more conciliatory tone, 'there's nothing personal in this. But there's something I should tell you. It's not a thing a father finds easy to tell. Still, for your own protection, you'd better know.'

Hugh stood in some unease and waited.

'You remember I told you she had a nervous break-down?'

'Yes. But she's all right now, isn't she?'

'What I didn't tell you was that she' – he hesitated, moving his head slowly from side to side – 'tried to take her own life.'

'My God,' Hugh gasped.

'We found her in the bathroom in pools of blood.' He covered his face with his hands and looked through his fingers to note Dolan's expression. The simpleton was as pale as a stick of blanched celery. 'Her wrists were slashed to here.' He pulled up his cuffs to demonstrate and was rewarded by a look of horror.

'That's terrible,' Hugh mumbled.

Ennis sighed. 'It isn't easy for a father to have to tell such things.'

'But she's better now, isn't she?' Hugh said again.

'She has her days,' he said enigmatically.

'It was that thing you were telling me about?' Hugh hinted delicately.

'Yes. That was it. That made a ruined girl out of her.' He looked appraisingly at Dolan, wondering how much further he should venture. 'Ruined!' he said again. 'Maybe you're surprised at me using a word like that? Maybe you think it too extreme? It might be, if you didn't know the full story.' He clenched his hands as if he were forcing himself to come to a decision. 'Look here,' he said eventually, 'you strike me as a decent fellow and not the kind to spread gossip. Do I have your word that you'll keep to yourself what I'm going to tell you now?'

'I swear to God I'll never say a word,' Hugh assured him.

'She's not . . . a virgin, you know. That damned fellow had his way with her.'

He watched with satisfaction as Dolan's face crumpled. He had been right in judging him to be a conventional fellow, easily shocked and likely to take the narrow, peasant view of a 'fallen' girl.

'Oh, yes,' he continued, 'ruined! I see you're shocked, and it does you credit. Any decent young fellow would be shocked. But what's done can't be undone and we'll have to live with it.' He knew that he had the fool on the run now. It would only take a short step to rout him altogether. 'Unfortunately there's more. It appears' – he stopped as if in great distress – 'it appears that – dammit! a father shouldn't have to say this – it appears that there was the pair of them in it. Anything that happened, happened by agreement.'

He looked at Dolan in pretended dismay. 'There, I've said too much, haven't I? Now you know it all – or nearly all.' He rounded on him roughly. 'How do I know you won't go blabbing this all over town?'

'I gave you my word,' Hugh whispered, his morale shattered. 'I'll never tell a soul. It's no business of mine.'

'No,' Ennis said. 'It's no business of yours.'

Taking this as a sign of dismissal, Hugh turned to go, but before he could leave, Ennis spoke again. 'You're wondering, now, why exactly all this drove her to do what she did. I' l tell you and then you'll know all there is to know. She became pregnant.' He stopped to savour the start this drew from Dolan. 'And what do you think our friend did then?'

'I don't know,' Hugh faltered.

'Denied all responsibility – that's what he did. Advised her that she should tell her family, or whoever was responsible – can you credit that? *Whoever was responsible!* – and get them to arrange an abortion.'

He watched the expressions that followed one another across Dolan's face. He noted revulsion, embarrassment, pity – and something more that might be interpreted as a determination to steer clear of this moral morass into which he had so nearly floundered.

'It was then,' Ennis continued, 'that she made her attempt.'

He watched as Dolan struggled to come to terms with this revelation. The hardest for him to take – the idea of putting it in had been a stroke of genius – would be her willing complicity. That should put an end to any romantic illusions he had been nourishing about her.

'There isn't much more to tell,' he added with feigned reluctance. 'You'll be wondering about the pregnancy and what came of that? Well, I'll tell you. It was the shock of – you know – the slashing of her wrists that brought it on. Anyway, a young fellow like you is as well not to hear all the details; the upshot of it was that she lost . . . she had a miscarriage.' He shook his head and squeezed his lips together in a tight line that bled his face white. 'Now you know everything there is to know. Now, maybe, you understand why I behaved as I did a while ago. Maybe you understand why – for your own sake and hers – I wasn't in favour of your dining here.'

Hugh nodded miserably. It all had obviously shaken him deeply.

'Well, that's life. All we can do is carry on.' Ennis looked at his watch. 'Time we were getting back to work.'

He opened the door and stood watching with a grim smile as Dolan slowly walked down the dark passage to the supermarket.

20 October 1980

He asked why I wasn't wearing the watch. Told him I'd taken it off to wash and had forgotten. Said he noticed I wasn't wearing it at dinner either. Told him she'd been enquiring about it. He said it was no business of hers and would I wear it or he'd be forced to think I didn't like it or was sulking about something.

Why hadn't she worn it? Why did she take it off when she was alone? She felt uncomfortable with it. She looked at it to see the time and saw something else instead.

She never wore it now when Hugh was about. How could she? Supposing he were to admire it and ask where it came from? Hugh was becoming important to her. He was normal. Cooking his dinner as well as she could and serving it as pleasantly as she could were normal activities. Talking to him about ordinary, everyday things was normal. Listening to what he had to say kept her in touch with normality.

Her mother had asked about the watch. It was the way she asked that gave offence – the accusing tone, the willingness to condemn. It was so expensive that, in her view, it constituted a bribe. She was right, of course. It was a bribe. But that was not why she had taken it. Sometimes, in spite of everything, she felt sorry for him. She had taken it to please him. She hadn't told her mother that. She was reluctant to acknowledge it to herself.

TWELVE

Could the blame for everything be laid at her door? Confessors were hard on women, she knew that from experience. It was the duty of wives to accommodate their husbands. It was their duty to lead them back from their carnal ways to the path of virtue. Father Simon had told her that she must return to her husband's bed. That was easy for him to say. What did he really know of marriage? What did he know of the degradation to which women are subjected?

When she went upstairs to look for Mary, she found her sitting at the dressing table in her room, writing in her diary. As soon as she entered the book was put away. There was something furtive about the manner of its hiding that continued to excite her curiosity.

'What are you writing?' She realised immediately that an interrogatory approach was not the best way to gain her daughter's confidence.

'Things,' Mary said evasively. She looked as if she had been crying.

'Sorry,' she said in a placatory tone. 'I wasn't meaning to pry. I just wanted to have a word with you.'

Mary was frequenting her room again. There must be some significance in that? She looked at her wrist and saw that the watch was missing. There must be some significance in that too.

'What is it?' There was no mistaking the defensiveness in Mary's voice.

It was not a very promising beginning. What was it in Mary that made her clam up like that whenever she tried to get through to her?

'I just wanted to talk,' she said. 'I was wondering if you had changed your mind about . . . anything?' She stopped, leaving the unspoken question dangling between them. She imagined, though she could not be sure, that for a second something flickered in Mary's eyes. It was enough to encourage her to stumble on. 'I mean – what I wanted to say was: it's never too late.' She stopped again as Mary turned away. She could not be sure whether the gesture signalled rejection or something else. Then she saw her hand brush her eyes. 'What I mean is – in spite of anything I may have said or done in the past – nobody blames you; nobody thinks any of this is your fault.'

Mary covered her face with her hands and collapsed into tears. Swiftly her mother crossed the room. She hesitated just a moment and then, awkwardly, she put her arms around the thin shoulders. They rested there for a second before they were shaken off with a little petulant shrug. She drew back, unsure of herself, the long years of hostility precluding closeness between them.

'I've been at fault,' she confessed painfully and with great effort. 'I haven't always been what I should have been to you – maybe, to him.'

The strain of that final acknowledgment was so distressing that she fell silent. She wondered if she really believed that to be true. Obviously Father Simon believed it. Sometimes it was easier to say a thing, to admit a fault – and in this case it had been anything but easy – than to *feel* responsible, to *feel* guilty.

'It's you,' she laid a hand tentatively again on Mary's shoulder, 'that I'm concerned about. You have your life in front of you . . . ' She felt the young body tremble. 'It needn't be like this always. There are things that can be done about it, if you . . . if only . . . if that's what you want.' She stroked the dark head gently and this time was not repulsed. 'You're not alone. Remember that,' she said.

Mary sniffed and began to wipe her eyes in a paper handkerchief that seemed to melt and disintegrate in her hands.

'You're upset now, so we'll say no more. We'll talk again later, if that's what you'd like. If you want help, will you come to me?'

She waited for a reply and was rewarded at length by Mary's nod. It was only a tiny movement, but it was enough to send her from the room in a spirit of hope.

How had it started? That was what she kept wondering. At some precise moment something happened, something was done, something was said, when something else should have been said or done or something else should have happened that would have prevented it all. The thing was somebody's fault. She kept thinking it was hers. She must have done something wrong.

It was when her body had begun to develop that things had changed. He seemed to look at her in a different way. He would put his arm around her and brush against . . . maybe touch. She had been uneasy. She hadn't liked it. She knew it wasn't an accident. But she had done nothing to stop it. She hadn't drawn away. She had been afraid that it might be an unfriendly thing to do.

Maybe it had all begun earlier. Even as a child she was in the habit of showing off in front of him. She was attracting attention to herself. She was putting temptation in his way. When he first came into her bedroom, she liked it. She was delighted. It was so cosy, so comforting.

When it did begin, she had let it happen. If she had said no, there might have been nothing. He hadn't been forceful at that time. Afterwards she had cried and pretended it had never happened.

She had come to hate her own body. She couldn't bear to look at herself any more. She hated her breasts and anything else about her that made him want to do what he did. She hated her face, if he liked it. She hated her hair, if it made him look.

She couldn't remember when she had stopped wearing perfume, doing herself up, caring about her appearance. She hadn't stopped doing it intentionally. It just happened. Something in her, some instinct, must have made her aware of what that kind of thing really was. It was laying yourself out to entice and entrap. She used to love painting her nails, trying out eye shadow, doing her hair in different ways just to see how it looked; she had spent hours before the mirror, plucking her eyebrows. Now she felt guilty. That was why she was so sure of her blame for everything. It was no use saying that she didn't know what she was doing, that she was too stupid. That was no defence. She was to blame for what she had done.

Hugh made no attempt at conversation beyond the bare civilities. He had been deeply distressed by what he had been told. He felt he had nothing in common with her, no subject on which he wanted to venture an opinion. He was afflicted by a mental numbness whenever he thought of her. He found her physical presence so disturbing that he could not focus his attention on anything else but her exact location in the room. He watched her covertly as she leaned over to place the meal in front of him. It was hard to believe that someone so young should have so much that was sordid and adult and ugly behind her.

When she smiled he wondered how she could ever have smiled again. He wondered, too, what he had been dreaming of to imagine that she might think of him. How gauche he must appear to her in comparison to that older man, who had so dominated her affections that she had been prepared to end her life on his account. He wondered what place the man now held in her mind and whether she still had suicidal thoughts.

When she stood beside him to serve his coffee, he found his eyes drawn to her wrists. They were thin, delicate . . . perfect. He saw the slender bones and tendons stretching down to her palms. He saw the blue veins; there were no scars – nothing but pale skin. Where were the scars that should have been there?

When she removed his cup, he had a chance to have another look. There was no mark that he could see on either wrist. They were as free from blemish as his own.

Whatever Mary had done, it was clear that she had not slashed her wrists. Perhaps she had threatened to do it and her father had exaggerated. But why should he? And why should he tell someone like himself, someone who was practically a stranger?

The problem occupied him for the rest of the afternoon.

There was no other one – no bad girl – to blame; there was only herself. One time, she had thought that if her mother were to acknowledge that the fault, or part of it, was hers, she could forgive her. But now that she had, Mary knew it wasn't true. The truth was that it was all her own fault – hers, and not someone else's, someone who could conveniently be loaded with her guilt.

Her father and mother had never been close, but nothing had happened until she interfered. Left alone they would have jogged along like two horses in harness, pulling against each other – uncomfortable, but not unbearably so.

What her mother was doing was asking Mary to forgive her, but she was the one who needed forgiveness. Mary had taken away any hope her mother had had of making things work out between them. She had taken away the uneasy compromise of that single bed, an arrangement that both had been learning to live with.

Her mother was human. She had touched her. The pity was that it came when she had forfeited any right to it. That was why she cried for hours. Her mother said it was not her fault. She meant well, but it was not true. She had wanted to apologise to her mother, but couldn't, because she didn't know how. It was as if her tongue had no flexibility to shape itself around the words. What words? She hadn't any.

What had her mother meant about change? She had said there were things that could be done. What could be done? Didn't she see that what had happened was irreversible? She was his. He believed she'd given him the right, and so she had. He wouldn't give up his right. He wouldn't let her go willingly. There was no compromise in him.

She had experienced so much in the past months that all her preconceived notions had turned out to be shallow and unreliable. It was too easy to see the surface and to see nothing beneath. It seemed to her that she had misjudged everybody. What did she really know about her mother? All she'd allowed herself to see was her reserve and her cold religion. It had never occurred to her that her mother might need a daughter as much as she needed a mother.

How was she to confide in her? If she were a little girl, she could have rushed into her arms. She had felt like doing just that, but had no words to go with it. All she could do was make sign language across a chasm, as if she belonged to some inarticulate tribe only lately come down from the trees.

Thinking of her mother brought her inevitably to him. The truth was that she had no father any more. All she had was this stranger who wanted her to be something she wasn't meant to be and had no wish to be. Where was her father? If he were there, he wouldn't allow her to be frightened. Nearly all the time now, especially at night, she was frightened. Her father used to come and wake her up and talk to her when she had nightmares. When she had nightmares now, she woke up wanting to scream. But she knew she shouldn't, because he might wake too and come looking for her. So she lay there, hardly breathing in case she disturbed him, and cried for her father – quiet crying with no sound, only the taste of bitter salt in her mouth. She cried because now her father had become her nightmare.

'There's a very sad thing,' Hugh ventured, when Mary appeared with his soup. He held out the *Record* and pointed to the headline: MOTHER DIES IN PLUNGE FROM BALCONY. She took the paper and smoothed it out. He watched her face intently while she read.

'They think it was suicide,' he said casually, his eyes hunting for a sign that never came. 'What would drive a woman to do a thing like that?'

'The loss of her baby, I suppose,' Mary said. There was compassion and sympathy in her voice – nothing more.

'It's a terrible way to take your life – if it was suicide.' He watched her narrowly as he repeated the word, but she did not flinch.

'It must have been a sudden impulse,' she said. The turn the conversation had taken did not seem to distress or embarrass her.

'It's less painful than . . . slashing your wrists, I suppose.' He studied her for reaction. There was none that he could see.

'She jumped off the balcony,' Mary reminded him.

'What I meant was that if I was to commit suicide I'd never do it by slashing my wrists. Would you?'

'No,' she said, 'or jumping off a balcony either.'

'How would you do it?' he asked, pushing the thing to the limit.

'I wouldn't do it at all,' she said after cool consideration. 'It's not fair . . . to the relatives. It leaves a mess for them to clear up. I wouldn't want that.'

It wasn't the kind of answer he had expected. It was all very strange. Did it mean that what her father had told him was not true? But why should he tell lies? Why should he blacken his own daughter and create suspicion about her stability? And if the suicide story was false, was the rest false too? He looked at the quiet girl and saw nothing that squared with any of the things her father had told him. There was something odd and unfatherly about the whole story.

'What's all this morbid talk about suicide?'

He looked up to see Mrs Ennis standing in the doorway.

'It was something in the paper,' Mary explained in a composed voice. 'A woman in Ballymun jumped off her balcony in a fit of depression after the death of her baby.'

'The poor thing! What happened to the baby?'

'It was one of those cot deaths. The baby was only six weeks old.'

He looked from one to the other in astonishment. Here they were, talking of a subject that should have been deeply distressing for both of them. Yet there was nothing in the manner of either to betray unease.

'She shouldn't have done it,' Mrs Ennis was saying. 'No matter how bad the situation, there's always hope.'

'She probably felt guilty,' Mary said.

'Sometimes people feel guilty who shouldn't,' Mrs Ennis said, 'and those who should, feel no guilt at all.'

There was an emphasis in the tone of their last exchange that suggested they might really be talking about something else. Mary looked away and quickly left the room.

In an attempt to learn more about that older man who had figured so dramatically in her past, he questioned his landlady. Mrs O'Brien could tell him very little except that Mary had always been a quiet, serious girl, unlike her brother Tom, who had a bad reputation about town and kept strange company and had gone off with some foreign hippies and never come back. She had heard from a girl down the street, who was a friend of Mary's – Angela, the youngest Curry girl – that she had left school suddenly and that was a surprise, because she was known to be a very bright student and there had been a piece about her in the *Record* the time she had won that writing competition. The essay had been printed in full – a very adult piece of work, not like a child's at all – with her photograph beside it.

She had never heard of her being delicate or sick, though she supposed she might have been, because that would certainly explain why she had been kept at home from school, wouldn't it? She had never heard of her name being linked with that of any man. What was she only a schoolgirl, after all?

Ennis was an odd, violent man – wild and brawling in his youth, as her husband could testify, both being of an age and schoolfellows together. His father had been a poor labouring man from Puddler's Alley, dead long since and all the rest of the family in America or England or God-knows-where, but all scattered these thirty years. Ennis had been a young improver like himself who married the boss's daughter. It created a stir at the time and there were the usual ugly rumours. But that was ridiculous because Sadie – that's Mrs Ennis – wasn't that kind of girl at all, or anything like it.

Hugh retired to his room. The puzzle was no nearer solution. All he could be sure of was that something traumatic had happened to Mary. Even though her father's account of it was neither sustainable nor credible in any of its circumstances that he had been able to check, it was clear from her general demeanour that she was unhappy.

THIRTEEN

Her success with Mary gave Mrs Ennis the courage to tackle her husband again. She had no illusions about the consequences, but she was bound to make the attempt. An opportunity presented itself, after tea, when Mary withdrew upstairs to her secret scribbling and left them alone.

He was seated at the table, sifting through a mound of paper and tapping out figures on his calculator. She knew he would resent being disturbed, but she was determined not to let the occasion slip.

'There's something I want to say.'

'Can't it wait?' he said without looking up. 'I'm busy.' There was an edge of irritation in his voice but, as yet, no more.

'No, it can't wait. But it won't take long.'

There was only one thing for her to do and, whatever happened, she was determined to do it.

He finished his calculations and looked up at her with dangerous calm. 'Well, what is it?'

'I just wanted you to know that I'm ready . . . to go back.'

'What do you mean go back? Go back where?'

'To being your wife,' she faltered. 'To do . . . anything you want me to do – a wife in the full sense.'

She watched as surprise, followed by a cynical sneer, crossed his face. 'Are you out of your mind?'

'I mean it,' she said. 'I'm serious. On condition –'

'Condition!' His voice was scathing. 'What condition? What makes you think I'd have you back or have anything to do with you on any condition? You're in no position to talk to me about conditions.'

'On condition,' she insisted, 'that you let Mary alone. That's the only condition I'll make.'

'The *only* condition!' He laughed harshly.

'I'll do anything,' she continued, in the face of his contempt, 'any of the . . . things you used want me to do. I mean . . . the whole lot – as often as you like.'

'You're ready to make a whore out of yourself?' he roared. 'You're ready to turn that bedroom upstairs into a knocking-shop? Is that what you mean?'

'There's no need to be coarse.'

'Aha!' he sneered. 'You're making rules already. We must be civilised about it, eh? In no time at all, you'd have us fuckin' to church music.'

'I know you're talking like that to put me off,' she said, 'but you won't put me off. I meant what I said. All I want is for you to leave Mary alone. You must see the damage you're doing to her.'

'Have you been at her again?' he challenged. 'Have you been upsetting her with your talk? By God, if you have, I'll burst you.'

'Do that and welcome,' she shouted, angry herself now, 'only leave Mary alone. I know I haven't been much of a wife in the past. I now see that the blame – part of the blame – for . . . what went wrong was mine.'

'The light on the road to Damascus!' he crowed.

'I never heard *you* acknowledge as much,' she retorted sharply, in spite of her determination not to be provoked.

'Now that you've made your gesture – some gesture!' – his tone was contemptuous – 'the answer is no!'

'We're talking about Mary's life – about her future.'

'I'll look after Mary better than you ever did,' he said. 'When have you ever done anything except push her away?'

'Do you call what you're doing *looking after* her? Do you expect me to accept that seducing her and corrupting her is *looking after* her?' she asked coldly. Her words might anger him, might be counterproductive, but how else, except by speaking the hard truth, could she bring him to a realisation of the injury he was doing to Mary?

'If you've finished,' he said curtly, 'I'll get on with my work.'

'Finished!' she shouted. 'No, I haven't finished and I never will finish until things are put right in this house. You're ruining your own daughter. You're degrading yourself. You're insulting and humiliating me. You're making a mockery of marriage. You're –'

'What marriage?' he roared. 'There never was any marriage. There was only denial and refusal and turning away. Don't you ever lecture me on marriage. To you marriage was never more than a mean little contract that gave you a manager for your business and freed you from the obligation of paying him a weekly wage.'

'I've paid dearly enough, then, in other ways and still am paying,' she said. 'What do you think all this is doing to me? What do you think I'm feeling? What do you think I'm suffering? I'm not made of stone. Have you ever thought how all this is going to end? How do you see Mary this time next year? How do you see her in five years' time? Still there to be used, without feelings or wishes or plans of her own? Is that how you see her? Your own daughter? A thing? An object? Something you can use and discard as you think fit? Not a person at all? Your property?'

'You wouldn't understand what's between Mary and me,' he said scornfully.

'Maybe not. It would take a psychiatrist to understand it fully. What I do understand is that it's wrong and must stop.'

'Must?' he asked sarcastically. 'Who'll make it? Not you for a start.'

'Maybe not, but I'll try.'

'Do,' he said with soft menace, 'but I'm warning you. Come in my way and you'll regret it.'

'I know what you're capable of. The whole town knew about that poor fellow you beat into a pulp.'

'It's nothing to what I'll do to you if you don't keep out of my way.'

'You'll have to kill me, then,' she cried, 'if you want to stop me.'

'If that's what you're looking for –' He jumped up and came towards her.

'Lay a finger on me,' she said, gaining courage from desperation, 'and I'll go straight to the priest and the guards and tell them everything.'

'Come on, then, before you change your mind.' He caught her by the arm and dragged her roughly down the hall to the front door, shouting, 'Tell the priests. Tell the guards. Tell the neighbours.' He opened the door and thrust her out. 'I'll call them for you. Get the guards. Call the canon. Here's a woman wants to make her confession.'

She stood without coat or hat in a torrent of rain and heard his manic shouts fill the empty street. They rang back at her from wet, reflective pavements and from the dark brow of buildings closed against the night.

'Stop it!' she pleaded. 'Stop!'

But he continued to shout, no more able to stop than a car horn that malfunctions.

'All right,' she said. 'You win – only stop for God's sake.'

The man was mad. He cared no more for Mary's reputation than he did for his own. She pushed at the door and tried to force her way in, but he thrust her out again, shouting, 'Stay there, damn you, and do your duty.'

He slammed the door and shot the bolt, and though she rang and knocked until her knuckles were raw, he would not let her in. The sleet came slanting in icy sheets, cutting through her thin dress. It beat off the pavement and hurled itself against the door. Her shoes were waterlogged. Her hair dripped in rat-tails. She could feel her skin creeping all down her body.

She darted through the entry at the side of the house and let herself into the yard by the latched gate. The kitchen was in darkness, the back door locked. What was she to do? She was shivering. Her clothes were a sodden mess. She rattled the knob and when there was no answer she groped blindly towards the garage, raised the door and let herself in.

There was a sudden calm when she closed the door. The

beat of water on the roof was a remote echo of the tumult outside. The air was warm with a heavy smell of oil. She felt around for the light switch and snapped it on, then wrung out the wet tails of hair that hung over her face and brushed them back. Using a clean piece of cotton rag that smelled of white spirit, she dried her hands and face.

She remembered the trunk of old clothes in the corner, and rooting through the cast-offs, found a tweed overcoat that she had worn as a young woman. It smelled of mildew and damp. It was long and voluminous and covered her to the ankles. She reached inside again and rummaged around until she found a green knitted hat, which she pulled on her head. After a while, her shivers became intermittent and she felt warmth seep back into her.

She turned off the light, raised the door and looked out. When her eyes became accustomed to the gloom, she saw the dark bulk of the house against the brightness from the street. In the yard a tail of water from a broken spout lashed and lapsed. She peered through the mesh of rain at the ground-floor lavatory window and stepped out into the weather, pulling the door down after her. The top section of the window was open, but it was too high for her to reach. She tried to climb up on the sill, but it was so wet that she slipped and grazed her knee. She stumbled around until she found plastic milk-crates stacked in a heap. She lifted one off, inverted it under the window, and stepped on it gingerly to test its strength. Then she stood up and reached inside to release the catch on the main casement, which swung open and allowed her to squeeze in.

He had challenged her to do her worst and she had failed the test. He had known her better than she knew herself. But she had to protect Mary from public exposure. She knew how rumour crept through those gossiping streets, fattening as it went. She knew of the scandal caused by illegitimate births and extramarital philanderings, of the hurried marriages for the sake of respectability, of the furtive trips abroad in search of abortion.

But it was her duty to seek help. To do that she would have to tell someone. But how could she ever, without dying of shame, tell another human being? It was one thing to hint at 'an unhealthy relationship' to Father Simon in the privacy of the monastery confessional. It was quite another to walk into the Garda barracks and tell her story in the bald language of the courts – for nothing less would be acceptable there – to Sergeant Evans and an audience of raw young guards.

She opened the door of the lavatory cautiously. If he saw her, he would be quite likely to put her out in the storm again. The corridor was empty. She tiptoed upstairs, took a towel from the hot-press in the bathroom, slipped into her bedroom and locked the door. She took off the musty hat and coat and stuffed them into a plastic bag. Then, standing in front of the mirror, her body twitching and shivering beyond control, her teeth grinding, she divested herself of her wet clothes and rubbed herself down with the towel.

She turned on the electric blanket on her bed and took up the towel again. In the mirror she saw her flabby, middle-aged, rejected body. With a shudder of distaste, she pulled on her heavy cotton nightdress and crept into bed.

When he went upstairs, Mary was waiting at the open door of her room.

'What's wrong? What did you do to her?' she asked.

'Never mind her. Come on to bed.'

'Where is she? Is she all right?'

'She was going to do the devil and all,' he said contemptuously. 'She's in her room like a drowned rat, if you must know. Now, come to bed.'

'I thought I'd sleep in here tonight. I don't feel well.' She looked at him with something like desperation, her eyes pleading that her simple fiction be accepted without question.

'Have you a headache?' It was impossible to keep the unsympathetic note out of his voice. It was an excuse that he had heard too often before.

'No. I just feel . . . rotten. I'll be all right in the morning.'

Something snapped inside him. He grabbed her by the hand and dragged her down the corridor. 'Getting just like her, aren't you?' He opened the door of his bedroom and pushed her in. 'Now,' he said, 'don't give me that rubbish she always gave me. Tell me what's wrong – and tell me the truth.'

'I'm not feeling well. That's all.'

'Is it your time or what?' he asked gruffly.

Gloom darkened in him as he watched her back away to the corner where that narrow single bed stood.

'No,' she said sullenly.

'What is it, then?'

Her attitude offended and enraged him. There was so much mistrust in those darting eyes, such fear in the crouch of her body that his heart sickened; it was as if she hated him. There was no hate in him for her, only love, nothing but love.

'Come on. Out with it.'

'I can't.' Mary stopped, tears flowing.

'Can't what?' He looked at her contemptuously, and waited.

'I can't . . . do it,' Mary cried.

He shook her violently. 'What do you mean? Can't or won't? Answer me.'

'Can't,' Mary trembled.

'There's no such thing as can't,' he roared. 'Why can't you?'

'Because . . . I forgot to take the pill.'

'When?'

'Yesterday. You said yourself we must never take chances.' She started to cry again – a steady unspectacular crying, cold and consistent, like winter rain.

He relaxed his grip and looked in surprise at the white print of his thumb on her arm. 'You should have told me.' He sat down on the bed, his large hands hanging between his knees.

'I was afraid you'd be cross,' she faltered. Then, hesitantly, rubbing her eyes and sniffing into a paper handkerchief, she asked, 'Can I go now?'

'You're in a great hurry to be off, aren't you?' he said morosely. He could see the tears swelling in her eyes again. Her reluctance excited him.

'Take off your clothes and get into bed,' he said.

'Couldn't I go?' Mary pleaded. 'Something might happen.'

'Damn that!' he shouted. 'Let's go to bed. Let's do something, for once, without being cautious and careful. To hell with the consequences.'

'I'd like to go. Please,' Mary pleaded.

Suddenly he knew beyond all doubt that the thing was

just a subterfuge to escape. 'You're a lying bitch, just like *her*. You didn't forget your pill. You haven't the spirit to finish what you started.' He struck her a sharp blow across the face.

'All right,' she shouted, as if instead of cowing her, the blow had given her courage, 'it is a lie. But that's your fault. I've been trying to tell you the truth for weeks now. But you don't want to hear it.'

'Try me,' he growled.

'The truth is . . . I want to stop.' Her voice trembled and fell to a whisper. 'I don't want to do those things any more.'

'She's been at you again, hasn't she?'

'It's what I want. It's nothing to do with anyone else.'

He reached for her and, when his hand brushed her thigh, something howled inside him at the thought of such loss. He felt her shrink away, her body hardening with rejection.

'I need you,' he said. Would she ever understand him at all? What he felt for her was not lust – whatever the moral-ists might call it. It was too basic, too primal for that.

'It's wrong,' she said. 'You know that.'

'It's not wrong when you can't survive without it.' He was removing her clothes as he spoke.

She struggled against him at first. Then a contemptuous indifference took over and she lay there, inert. When he tried to kiss her, she resisted. Brutally he beat her with closed fists and forced himself on her, until she collapsed and lay whimpering under him.

When he had finished, he tried to take her into his arms, but she pushed herself away and lay cold and hard as a stone, no longer sobbing, her eyes open and staring, their focus somewhere beyond the walls of that room. He drew her underneath the blankets and quenched the light. It was unbearable to look any longer at those blank, loveless eyes.

It seemed to him that the cycle of his life had run full circle and was beginning to repeat itself. What he felt now he had felt before. How many times had he lain like this with a cold, unresponsive body beside him? How many nights had he lain at the other side of a wall of silence, his mind on the past? What had gone wrong? He would have to take her away. Once out of the place she would allow that hedonistic part of her nature, which she had shown in the early days, to come into its own again.

He stretched out his hand to touch her. Again she shrank from him. An idea floated into his mind, a disturbing idea that had circled about him like a wasp many times already. Could there be something between her and that greenhorn, Dolan? Dolan was a clumsy lout. But she . . . she was experienced now. She could be the initiator.

'Tell me,' he cried in agony, 'what's changed?'

There was movement, but she did not speak. The movement itself was an answer. It was away from him.

'I know,' he said with contrition, 'I was rough and I'm sorry. I love you. Hurting you is the last thing I want. But when you're like that, I do things I'm sorry for. You should know me by now. You shouldn't provoke me. It only happens when you're not honest with me, and then I suffer for it. I'm suffering now. Don't you know that?'

A steadfast silence was her only answer.

'Is there someone else?' he asked. 'Is it that fellow?'

There was movement in the bed again, agitated movement, as if she were attempting speech, but his straining ear could catch no sound.

'Don't be afraid. I want to know the truth.'

The answer came, faint but firm. 'I've told you the truth. I want to stop, because it's wrong. It should never have started. I'm sorry it did.'

'It is that fellow, isn't it?' he said.

'It's nothing to do with anyone else.'

'Nothing at all? Nothing to do with that snivelling Dolan?'

'Nothing.'

'You don't even like him, I suppose?' he said bitterly. 'You never go out of your way to talk to him? You say more to him than you ever say to me. I've heard you. I've listened. I've watched. I've seen you – and then you expect me to believe there's nothing.'

'I didn't know it was wrong to talk . . . ' she began coldly.

'I heard you laughing too. You never laugh with me.'

'There isn't much to laugh about,' she whispered and started to cry again.

'We'll go away,' he said. 'Everything will be all right once we get away from this cursed house. What do you say?'

'I just want to go back to my room and be like I was before.'

'But why?' he said. 'What's gone wrong?'

'We should never have done what we did,' she said. 'I'm sorry about my part in it. I'm sorry if it was anything I was, or I did, that made you want me like that. It's all my fault. If I wasn't the kind of person I am, it wouldn't have happened. I feel so ashamed and guilty. Please, let me go back to my own room. I want us to be like we were before.'

She began to sob softly. 'I want you to be my father.'

That relationship, he told himself, was over and done with. It belonged to childhood. 'We can never go back,' he said. 'What has happened can't be changed. You and I have a new relationship.'

'No!' she protested. 'I'm your daughter. You're my father. That's the only relationship I want between us. You say you love me. If you did, you wouldn't want to force me –'

'So I forced you, now, did I?' he said angrily.

'What would you call what just happened?' she replied with spirit.

'I'm talking about the first day. You were agreeable then, and you've no right to go back on it now. You and I are stuck with each other – for better or worse.'

'For better or worse!' she exclaimed. 'I thought that had to do with a promise you made long ago – and to some-body else.'

'You've no call to drag that into it. That's over and done with. The past is dead. Let it rest. You and I are the future.'

'So, what I think and what I want don't matter at all?'

She started to cry again, a slow-paced, steady crying.

FOURTEEN

Afterwards he had been full of remorse, but what went before was so horrible that she was numb and bruised and angry – hard, too, and unforgiving, wanting him to suffer the way he had made her suffer.

Everything he said was contradictory. He pretended to be her protector, when the one person she needed protection from, the one person he couldn't or was unwilling to protect her from, was himself. He talked about what happened long ago being his inspiration – about it being a light to guide him – when it was more like a will-o'-the-wisp, leading him astray. Now he expected her to carry his dream.

Could she ever again live normally? He had his pleasant memories to keep him going – a sunny day and that girl. But what memories had she? She only wanted to forget, and how was she to forget? Every waking hour was pain to her, and at night she had fearful dreams.

He was jealous of Hugh, thinking there was something between them. Hugh was her friend – that was all. She liked him because he was normal. He had no guilty secrets, no shameful past or present. The sun rose clear and bright for him. He looked at it and had nothing to hide.

She'd never let herself be taken away. He thought a change of scene would make a difference. What was wrong between them had nothing to do with where they were, but with what they were, and going away wouldn't change that.

What was it about her that still attracted him? She'd done her best to make herself unattractive. It could hardly be her clothes. She never wore a dress any more. She had made a beautiful dress for herself in the spring and been very proud of it. He had said it was nice. Was it then that it all had begun?

He lay awake and wondered what had gone wrong. It was not his wife's finding out. For him part of the satisfaction was that she should know and that her love of respectability should prevent her from taking action. That was the ultimate irony: that his own wife should now be an accessory to incest.

'Are you awake?' he whispered to Mary.

There was no reply. He listened. Her breathing was shallow, controlled. She was awake, holding her breath.

'I know you can hear me. Things will mend when we get away. You'll see.'

A slight change in her breathing was the only sign that she had heard.

'I'd be better to you. I'd be more relaxed. There wouldn't be anybody to get me worked up and make me lose my temper. What do you think?'

Again there was no reply.

'Things have got so bad that I can't stand the super-market. All I can think about – or want to think about – is you and how we're to solve this problem that's facing us. We have to solve it or it's the end of the road for me. All my life I've waited for this thing. I was never even remotely near to finding it until you came along. I know it all goes against convention and what people think of as being right. But convention is only whatever people agree that it should be. There's no absolute right or wrong. Why shouldn't it be possible for us to have a loving relation-ship? It's not doing any harm to anyone else. Nobody can say it's doing harm to her. She opted out of any relation-ship, so how can she complain? I didn't abandon her. She abandoned me.'

He stretched out his hand in reconciliation and felt her draw away.

'I'm sorry,' he said. 'Please forgive me. I was afraid – I'm not making excuses, I'm only trying to explain. You know that I can't do without you. That's your great trump card. But you'll have to learn how to play it.'

If he expected any response out of that hurt silence, he got none. It was so still that he fancied he could hear the dust settle in distant corners. At intervals he resumed his monologue, ranging through his life. He told her about his childhood, about the father who had beaten and brutalised him, about the mother who had cheated him by dying when he was ten years old. He remembered, in particular, how he had been hurt by that betrayal, how he had raged against it, how he had knelt at her bed and pleaded with her to wake up and not abandon him like that, how he had caught her cold stiff hands and tried to pull her back, how in despair he had flung a stone into her grave and how he still remembered the ring it made against the brass plate of her coffin.

He told her how his father had given him into the care of an uncle and gone off to England, from where he had returned some years later with a strange woman, whom he had introduced as his wife. After a short stay they had gone back and he hadn't been troubled by them again. Years later, news had come from a midland town that his father was dead. The news had meant nothing to him.

He told her things there in the darkness that he had never told to anyone before. Whether she heard or not he was no longer sure. All he knew was that there was a kind of relief in talking. It seemed to him that if he could tell her everything, she would understand him, she would appreciate that, at heart and in his inner core, he was a gentle and a loving man.

She and her mother talked now – just enough to constitute a conspiracy. They were, at least, on the same side, though they hadn't spoken much about that. Maybe it was a sense of shame on their part; maybe it was just helplessness. What could they do? She supposed, for a start, they could discuss that very thing. But it took time to build trust. The two of them had been like aliens, uncomfortable in each other's presence, for most of her life. They had to learn how to communicate. It must be very hard for her mother, whose whole life had been laid bare – her inadequacies, her failures. His turning to her had been a rejection of her mother. Not only was she instrumental in it, but she was privy to her mother's most painful secrets.

20 November 1980
Told her I wanted it to end, and that did something to ease things
between us. Told her I was afraid. She's afraid too, especially
after the night he put her out in the rain. Said I must tell him,
however hard it was going to be. Told her I'd tried.

She despised herself for being so cowardly. She'd always
prided herself on telling the truth. Now he'd even taken
that from her.

She could run away. She could go to Tom, if she knew
where he was. But what help would he be? She'd have to
do it on her own, relying on nobody, not even her mother.
That way he couldn't take it out on her when she was
gone. She could go to Dublin and get a job there. Dublin
was a dangerous place these days, but what could anyone
do to her there that hadn't already been done to her at
home?

There had been no communication between them since
that terrible evening. When she had taken to her bed, it
was Mary who had looked after her. She had wrapped her
in blankets and nursed her until she recovered.

Mary was changing. Her manner was no longer hostile.
There was a humility about her, a willingness to please.
She had brought in chrysanthemums from the garden
and arranged them in a vase. Mrs Ennis was touched by
the gift. The poor girl looked pale and uncared for. She
seemed to camp out in her clothes rather than inhabit
them, like a tramp in an empty house.

'I thought you'd like those,' she said.

'They're beautiful.'

Their beauty went far beyond the display they made. She put out her hand in a gesture of thanks, but Mary, shy of such demonstrativeness, stood at a distance, looking as if she had something to say and didn't know how to begin.

'You've been thinking things over, haven't you?' her mother prompted.

'I've told him I want it . . . to finish. But it didn't do any good.'

Her mother saw the tears gathering in her eyes. 'Thank God!' she said, and felt her own eyes dim. She heard with growing impatience the account of his maudlin monologue, breaking in to exclaim, 'On about her again, was he? Sooner or later, if things get bad enough, or he's drunk enough, he'll come to her. She's his excuse for every mean and selfish thing he's turned his mind and his hand to since he was a boy. It's all lies, you know. If it happened at all, it certainly wasn't the kind of encounter he makes it out to be – all joy and innocence and summer light.'

'How do you know?' Mary asked.

'I knew her, or, at least, I knew of her. A lot of people knew of her, she was that kind of girl. Her people were a wild, dark crowd – drinking, brawling men and slatternly women, doing a day's washing here, a day's cleaning there, the guards around on a Saturday night, broken glass and fights on the street. Now you see what rubbish that man has been inventing for the last thirty years. Sooner or later that one is paraded as a model of all the virtues. It's pathetic when you think of the reality.'

When she was up and about again, she sat in the kitchen and watched Mary come and go, serving Dolan's meals.

His presence there, young and male and wholesome, was still useful.

'He's a nice quiet boy,' she observed, 'the sort a girl like you should be interesting yourself in.' She watched in dismay as tears began to swell in Mary's eyes. 'What's wrong?'

'You know what's wrong. My life is over.'

'Nonsense! You must put all this behind you. You must go back to being the girl you were. You must take up the interests you had. You must seek out the company of young people of your own age.'

'How can I?' Mary let the tears flow unchecked. 'Who'd want to know me? Who'd want to have anything to do with me if they knew the kind I was?'

'You did nothing wrong.'

'You didn't always think that.'

'No – and I'm sorry. Nothing would have happened if he hadn't made it happen. You're the injured one and you could be done a further injury if the thing became known. That's why we can't go to the guards. I only wish we could. I've thought of doing it a thousand times.'

'What can we do?' Mary wailed.

'We'll think of something,' her mother said, with an optimism she was far from feeling. She watched as Mary dried her eyes. In an attempt to cheer her up she continued, 'You could do with some new clothes. You're beginning to neglect yourself, and we'll have to do something about your hair.'

'What effect do you think that's going to have on him?' Mary burst out passionately. 'Do you think new clothes and a hairdo is going to make him leave me alone?'

'No, child,' her mother said. 'I don't. But if you've got

the notion that by being dowdy and careless and neglecting yourself he'll lose interest in you, I'm afraid you're mistaken. You must remember he doesn't see you at all. It's that other slut he sees – and he sees her exactly as he wants to see her. I'm sure she wasn't too clean or too particular about herself.'

Mary sat at the table, supporting her head with her hands. Her tossed hair covered her fingers to the knuckles.

'The coffee,' she said. 'I can't take it in looking like this.'

'I'll do it,' her mother said. 'You go upstairs and rest.'

Hugh was reading the newspaper when she went in.

'I'm afraid we forgot your coffee,' she said.

'That's all right, ma'am.' He folded his paper neatly and laid it on the table. 'I hope I didn't upset Mary the other day,' he said.

'Why would you upset her?' she asked, wondering what had been said.

'All that talk of suicide – the woman who threw herself off the balcony . . . '

'Why would that disturb Mary, in particular?'

'After what happened . . . and all,' he said lamely.

'What do you mean *after what happened*?'

Hugh blushed with embarrassment. 'It was something Mr Ennis told me.'

'What did he tell you?' All her suspicions were aroused.

'About that man . . . and all.' He spilled his coffee in his agitation.

'Go on,' she said grimly. 'What man?'

'The one she was friendly with.'

'What did he say about Mary and this man?'

'He said that she'd got . . . into trouble –'

'What!'

' – and that was why she left school and had tried to' – he hesitated in embarrassment – 'to slash her wrists.'

'Oh, my God! My husband told you that? There's not a word of truth in any of it. There was no man. Mary's never been out with anybody in her life. She's never been in trouble or done anything wrong like that – ever. Slashed her wrists! You didn't believe him, did you?'

'I didn't know what to believe,' Hugh confessed in confusion.

'He didn't want you talking to her – that's what it was. He'd rather blacken her character than let her talk to boys. If he had his way, she'd never talk to anybody. I hope now that you know the truth you won't allow anything he said to affect your opinion of her.'

'Of course not,' he said warmly. 'I always thought her a grand girl.'

FIFTEEN

When he went into dinner, Hugh was carrying a shoe box with air holes in the lid, which he placed carefully on the floor beside his chair. Mary came in and busied herself about the table, setting out mats and cutlery. He spoke to her and she replied in her usual diffident manner, not looking directly at him but slightly to the side. He watched her long fingers arranging the cutlery, and realised that he could look at her now without any feeling of uneasiness. A protective, jealous father was something he could cope with.

He looked down at the shoe box and wondered if he should wait until the end of the meal. A sound of scratching came from inside. He lifted a corner of the lid and peeped in, and was about to replace it when he saw Mary looking at him. He held out the box to her and tried to speak casually. 'A little present for you. I thought you might like it.'

She took the box and lifted the lid carefully. A marmalade kitten with a white throat and ringed tail eased himself out and climbed to her shoulder, purring and rubbing himself to her cheek.

'He's beautiful,' she said, taking him in her arms and stroking until the purrs came up strong and vigorous. 'Thank you very much.' Her eyes were glistening as she held the kitten to her cheek and turned away. 'When was he fed?' she asked.

'This morning,' Hugh said. 'A little milk is all he needs.'

'What's his name?' she asked, combing her fingers along the kitten's back and up the sweep of his curved tail.

'You'll have to christen him yourself.'

He watched with a smile as she carried him out to the kitchen. She returned with his soup to announce that the kitten was drinking milk and enjoying himself hugely. Her manner was more open. She was more willing to talk and to linger in the room when her work had been completed.

She was not at all the kind of girl he had dreamed about in adolescence. He had dreamed of uncomplicated girls, beautiful and carefree, who would wander, laughing, with him through summer woods. Mary was sad and introverted, with unfathomable depths in her dark eyes.

When he came back the following day, there was a bowl of chrysanthemums on the table, warm and russet against the white cloth.

'For you,' she said.

He bent to smell them and in his awkwardness almost overturned them. They both put out hands to save the flowers and laughed self-consciously at their own gaucherie.

'How is the kitten?' he asked, when the flowers were rescued.

'Fine. I made a little bed for him in the kitchen in an old doll's house. He sleeps and eats and plays and enjoys life.

It must be nice to be a kitten.'

He caught the tone of wistfulness and smiled sympathetically. 'Have you found a name for him yet?'

'I thought I'd call him Tuesday − after the day you gave him to me.'

'That would amuse my mother,' he said. 'I got him from her, you know.'

'What would your father think?'

'My father is dead. We found him in the field, sitting beside a half-made cock of hay with his pipe in his hand. His fingers were like ice, even though it was a hot summer's day. My mother was never the same after it.'

They fell silent, preoccupied with their thoughts, then Mary went back to the kitchen. He hadn't spoken about his father for years. He had been twelve when they found him. Men in hay fields had troubled him ever since.

When he was drinking his coffee, Mary returned and silently laid an envelope on the table and fled. He looked at it curiously. It was addressed to himself. He slipped the handle of his teaspoon under the flap and burst it open. Her handwriting was neat and precise, running in ordered lines across the unruled page.

Dear Hugh,

The kitten is beautiful. I can't think of anything that could give me more pleasure. I'm going away soon − I'd like to have a job and be independent − and I'll take it with me. It will be the one happy memory I'll have of this place, something I can always associate with you and your cheerful presence.

There's a problem about leaving and I'm hoping you may be able to help. I don't want anyone here to know where I'm going or when, so I can't ask for money. I have none and no way of making any, but I do have a valuable watch which should easily fetch fifty pounds if I could pawn or sell it. I know you go to Dublin sometimes on your day off and I was wondering if you'd take it with you next time you go and see what you can get for it.

Please let me know if you can help. I'll always be grateful to you.

Mary

He put the letter in his pocket and went back to work, his mind full of speculation. Why was she leaving and where did she intend to go? It was clear that she regarded herself as a prisoner in that house. What was wrong with her father, anyway? There was no problem in getting to Dublin. His former employer made the journey early on Wednesday mornings, returning late the same night with a van load of goods for his store. Hugh had been his helper and still went with him occasionally.

After work he sat in his bedroom with a lined writing pad in front of him and bit the end of his biro in search of the right words. He wasn't used to writing letters. In the end – because he knew of no other way – he wrote in the bald, prosaic manner in which he spoke.

Dear Mary,

Of course I'll help. I'll take the watch with me next Wednesday and pawn it for you. If you like I could lend you the fifty pounds or even a hundred. I have some money saved and could draw it out at any time. I hope you have friends to go to and that you'll be well looked after. I'm glad you like the kitten. If you wrote to me at my digs and let me know where you were I could maybe go and see how he was coming along if that's all right. I wouldn't tell anyone here where you were.

Your sincere friend,
Hugh

He slipped her the letter next day at lunch time, and watched as she folded it inside her handkerchief and went into the kitchen. Ten minutes later she was back to lay the watch on the table beside him. 'Put it in your pocket. I don't want anyone to know.'

He picked it up, glanced at it long enough to see that it was expensive, and put it away. 'Fifty pounds – is that it?'

'Yes. Whatever you can get.'

'It's a very good watch. It might be nice to have some day.'

'I hate it,' she said. 'I never want to see it again.'

He was surprised at her vehemence. 'I'll try and make the best deal I can. If I can't get enough, I'll lend you the money myself – more than fifty, if you like.'

'Thank you.' She was visibly moved. 'But I'd rather sell the watch.'

'Whatever you like. I'll see what I can do on Wednesday.'

She thanked him and went off to fetch the rest of his meal. When she came back, he asked where she intended going.

'Dublin, but you mustn't tell anybody.'

'Maybe we'll meet some Wednesday,' he said. 'I could call to see you.'

'I'll let you know,' she said. 'I'll write.'

'I'd like that,' he said.

When he was drinking his coffee, she brought in the kitten and set it on the table. It tiptoed with arched back and curved tail between the plates, mewing and purring. He poured a little milk into his saucer and held it out. They watched, smiling, as it settled down to lap the milk, its tiny tongue, pink and curved, darting in and out.

Behind them in the doorway, unobserved, stood the benign figure of Mrs Ennis. Behind her, the door to the shop opened noiselessly and the dark shadow of her husband filled the passage.

Tuesday sat beside her, pawing at the pen as she wrote, rubbing himself against her hand. He was lovely. When they went away, she'd have to find a place where they liked cats and would look after him while she was working.

There was no way of ending the thing except by going. He was getting worse all the time. He expected her to please him more. She never wanted to do any of those things again. She didn't want anyone to look at her, or touch her, or like her, that way. She never wanted to get married. She wanted to live alone with her kitten and forget. Hugh could come and see her. He was different.

She couldn't tell her mother about going. It would only make things more difficult for her. She felt so sorry for her now, so guilty about her own behaviour – not just this, but all those years of passing judgement. She still didn't find it easy, she still hadn't found a way, to love her. She just felt sorry for her and sorry for herself, because there were no strands with their roots burrowing back into the past to bind them together. It was her hope that this mess might end by bringing them closer. She had arrived at the stage where she felt the need of her. Sometimes at night she lay awake and thought of what it would be like to have had that special kind of relationship all through her childhood, warm, close, intimate. She saw the attraction of that now.

His wife was in the kitchen when he came in to tea. He glanced at her sourly and sat down at the table. Words were no longer adequate, or necessary, for communication between them. Looks, grunts, sighs, snorts of derision were sufficient to tell how little they approved of – how intolerant they were of – each other. He took a swift look through the newspaper and tossed it aside, then cut himself a slice of bread, speared a lump of butter and smeared it on carelessly.

She stood by the cooker and arranged rashers and sausages on a plate. She left them on the counter and removed her apron. She was prepared to cook but not to serve his meals. He watched her wash her hands and dry them. The woman was so damned methodical and predictable. He waited for her to open the door and go out in her usual fashion, without a word or a backward glance. Instead, she turned and stood, a contemptuous look on her face.

'What lies have you been telling about Mary?'

'What are you talking about?'

'It was despicable to tell young Dolan that she tried to kill herself.'

'You should have seen the fool,' he grated harshly and without embarrassment. 'Couldn't back off fast enough. It's you should be ashamed – wanting to tie your daughter to a snivelling chancer like that.'

'He knows now it was all lies. So there's no more harm you can do in that line.'

'Maybe I'll have to tell him the truth.'

'You wouldn't,' she cried, the whole façade of her confidence crumbling.

'Wouldn't I!' He looked at her without pity. 'Why didn't *you* tell him?' he taunted. ''Twas your duty, wasn't it?'

She said nothing. He turned away in disgust from her grey, bent head. He picked up the slice of bread from his plate and crumpled it between his palms. He got up and dropped it into the waste bin. Lifting the plate of rashers and sausages from the counter, he dumped them in on top of it.

From the doll's house the kitten daintily stepped out, its nostrils quivering, and walked with arched tail to inspect the bin, crying as it went. It stood on its hind legs and reached upwards towards the lip. Ennis looked at it.

'Where did that kitten come from?'

Mrs Ennis rushed to pick it up. Before she could, he had grabbed it by the folds of skin about its neck and held it up to inspect it.

'Give him to me. He's Mary's.'

'So that's what was going on!' he shouted angrily. 'Giving her presents now, is he?' He recalled the previous day, the sound of laughter, the open door, his wife standing beside it, a complacent smile on her face.

'It's just a little kitten,' she said, suddenly fearful. 'It meant nothing. Here, give it to me.'

'You encouraged this.' He held out the kitten as proof of her complicity. 'You thought you were being very clever, didn't you?' He shook the kitten violently, breaking its cries of fright into shrill fragments.

'You'll hurt it. Give it to me.' She stretched out to snatch it from him.

He held his hand higher and pushed her away, then turned to the sink, plugged the hole and turned on the water.

'No,' she shouted. 'No.'

He watched the water dispassionately as it swirled into the sink, covering the bottom and climbing the sides. An ice-cold anger filled him. His wife's protests only strengthened his determination. He held the kitten over the water, waiting. The water bubbled and swirled and mounted.

His wife ran shouting into the hall. 'Mary, come quick! Come quick!'

She seized a knobbed walking stick from the hall stand and rushed back, then raised the stick and brought it down on his shoulders. He turned with a shout of pain, and still holding the kitten in his left hand, lunged at her. She lifted the stick again with both hands. As it came down he brushed it aside with his forearm and it slid harmlessly away.

Before she could raise it again, he grabbed it, threw all his weight behind it, and sent her crashing backwards on the floor. It was his turn to raise the stick then. She put up her hands to protect her head and tried to roll beyond his reach. He stood a second with the stick poised in his right hand and looked at her, then with a roar he brought it down with all his strength on the floor beside her. The stick broke in two. He threw the jagged piece he held in his hand into a corner and turned back to the sink. On the floor his wife whimpered and pulled herself into a sitting position by the wall. Upstairs, a door opened and there was the sound of running feet.

Mary burst into the kitchen and ran to help her mother. Then she saw her father with the kitten poised over the water.

'No!' she screamed. 'No!'

He plunged the kitten into the water, holding it under by the soft folds of its neck. Little bubbles of air rushed from its fur, which stood out like a ruff around its body, and floated to the surface. The pink pads of its feet made swimming motions, clawing at the water for support. He watched coldly as its mouth moved in little submerged, mewling cries, its white teeth stripped and bare.

'Don't!' Mary screamed. 'Please, don't!'

She pulled at his arm, rigid and inflexible as a rod of iron. She made a sudden dart to snatch at the plug chain, but he stopped her. He watched in a clinical way as the kitten struggled for life. He felt it shiver and tremble in his hand. He watched the tiny head, the fur sleeked back, smaller now, and more slender. Its movements were sluggish, drowsy, its feet moved more slowly. The string of bubbles rising from its nostrils came broken, smaller, more and more intermittent.

Mary beat at him with her hands, crying to him to stop, pleading with him, begging. He neither looked nor spoke. The kitten's fur clung to its body now, its pale skin visible underneath. He held it still, feeling slight quiverings and tremors through his rigid fingers. The lips were stripped back from the teeth, pressed down and blanched. The body tilted sideways and away from him. The legs twitched in a dying spasm and from the open mouth tiny quicksilver beads emerged and clung to teeth and lips before floating off through the translucent water. He relaxed his grip and the body drifted free.

Turning away, he caught the hands that were still beating at him. He held her by the wrists and looking through her, said, 'You'll take presents only from me. Let this be a lesson to you.'

He unlocked her hands and walked out of the room. He heard the suck and whirl of water from the sink, the cries of his daughter as she lifted the kitten's body. He took his overcoat from the hall stand and went out to walk the streets.

The air was crisp and sharp. A thin wind, laced with frost, met him at street corners. The ground was crunchy underfoot. The light from the lamps was coldly edged with blue, like Arctic sunlight. He turned away from town and headed towards the country.

Why, he raged, did she betray him like that? Every turning away from him to someone else was a betrayal. Every thought that did not include him was a betrayal. Every desire that went beyond him was a betrayal.

He stood on the edge of town and looked over the bridge at the shallow water of the Coorbane river, sliding into the blackness beneath him. A thin, stinging wind whipped over the parapet. The surface of the water was broken by projecting stones that combed it out into long tresses.

He would have to take her away. But where could he take her so that she would be safe from interference? Wherever they went, there would be Dolans to give her presents and seduce her away from him.

He walked out to the cross and took the steeply

ascending road that brought him round in a wide loop until he was looking down at the wintry lights of the town. Somewhere in there, beyond Paupers' Acre, was the place where it had all begun. He stood looking down, his arms folded across a wooden gate, until the cold entered into him.

Mrs Ennis looked at Mary, sitting there with the dead kitten in her arms. She was drying the body with a towel, dabbing the flattened fur and the sleek head, pressing the chest and holding it with head lowered to let driblets of water leak from the open mouth. She felt with her fingers for a pulse. Then she began dabbing at the limbs again, drying the pads of the feet and between the extended claws.

Her mother stood beside her and put her arms about her shoulders. 'We'll have to get you away from this house.'

'Its poor body is cold,' Mary said, 'cold as ice.'

'It's dead, child. Here, let me take it from you.'

Mary turned away, holding it closer to her. 'I thought I felt a little stir. Maybe a hot-water bottle . . . '

'We can try,' her mother said, with an optimism she did not feel. She found a rubber hot-water bottle in a press underneath the sink and filled it from the hot tap. She dried it carefully and brought it over. She put the bottle on the table and Mary laid the towel-wrapped body on top of it. Her mother looked at her and then at the kitten and then at Mary again. 'The kitten is dead, child,' she said tearfully. 'Can't you see that? What we have to think of now is getting you away from here.'

'I am going away,' Mary said in a quiet, dispassionate

voice. 'But I'll make my own arrangements.'

'What arrangements?'

'It's best you don't know. That way, he can't make you tell him.'

'You know I wouldn't tell him,' her mother protested.

'I know you wouldn't *want* to. But I know now the kind of person he is.'

'I can help you with money.'

'He might find that out, too. I don't want him to have anything that he can use against you. I'll be all right. Trust me.'

Mary turned back to open the blanket and look at the kitten's body. 'He killed my kitten,' she said, and the tears began to fall silently.

'I shouldn't have called you, child,' her mother said. 'It wasn't a thing for you to see. I only did it because I thought you'd be able to stop him. I thought he had some regard for you and would spare it for your sake.'

'It's my fault he's dead,' Mary said. 'I should never have taken him. I ought to have known.' She lapsed into tears again.

'What are you going to tell Hugh?'

'I'll tell him the truth – or as much of it as I can.'

When lunch time came round again, Mrs Ennis stood near the door, trying to overhear their conversation, but all she could make out was the quiet murmur of Mary's voice and subdued responses from Dolan.

'Well?' she enquired when Mary returned.

'He said he could get me another.' Mary brushed her eyes tearfully.

'If only everything could be settled as simply as that,' her mother said.

SIXTEEN

Hugh was restocking shelves when Ennis spoke behind him.

'I want a word with you.' There was a hard edge to his voice and a harder set to his face.

'I want a word with you too,' Hugh said in the same hostile tone. 'It's about that kitten.'

'It's about the kitten I came.' Ennis spat the words out harshly.

'You had no right to drown it.'

'You had no right to bring it into my house.'

'What harm could there be in giving her a kitten?'

'Two harms.' Ennis thrust his face aggressively closer. 'For a start, you were hired to work here, not to make up to the daughter of the house.'

'I wasn't making up to her,' Hugh said angrily.

'The second is this: that girl is allergic to cats. She's always been allergic to cats. I told you she was delicate. That cursed kitten wasn't two hours in the house when it sparked off an attack of asthma – something to do with the fur. Dammit, I told you the girl was delicate.'

'You told me a lot of things, but they weren't true,' Hugh grated. 'You told me she slashed her wrists. That wasn't true.'

'Slashed – threatened to slash – what's the difference!'

'She never did anything like that. Mrs Ennis told me.'

'What do you expect her mother to tell you – an outsider and a stranger?' Ennis sneered. 'Now, I'm telling you this. Keep away from that girl. I don't want to see you talking to her or interfering with her again.'

'I wasn't interfering with her,' Hugh said flatly.

'I know you,' Ennis said. 'I know what you're after.'

'You think I'm after all this, I suppose.' Hugh took in the supermarket with the sweep of his hand. 'But you're wrong. If I ever own a business, I won't be beholden to anyone for it. I'll work for it and pay for it too. When I get married I won't be marrying because the girl has property, but because she wants me and I want her.'

As he turned away to go back behind the counter, suddenly shy after such a long and self-revelatory speech, he felt Ennis's hand heavy on his arm.

'Just a minute! I haven't finished yet. You're a very independent fellow, so you won't mind making your own arrangements about lunch from now on. You'll not eat here or trouble my family again. Is that understood?'

'All this fuss because I gave her a kitten!' Hugh shouted. 'Did you have to kill it in front of her?'

He braced himself behind the counter as Ennis snatched a hammer from a rack beside him and raised it above his head. He was poised to strike when the doors opened and two women came in. They picked up baskets and began to move among the shelves. Ennis, his face red with anger, lowered the hammer and leaned across the counter to hiss, 'Talk to me like that again and I'll smash your skull.' He replaced the hammer and marched stiffly back to his station.

A few days later, when Ennis had gone indoors for lunch, Hugh watched Mary coming towards him down the supermarket, her dark hair tumbling. Selling the watch hadn't been easy. The truth was that he hadn't been able to sell it at all. Wherever he had gone he had been looked at suspiciously. Was the watch his? Where had it been bought? Why was he selling it? The questions were sometimes asked bluntly; sometimes they hung in the air like an unspoken accusation. It was easier in the end to withdraw seventy pounds from his account and keep the watch as a memento. He might be able to return it to her one day.

Mary smiled nervously as she approached. He had the money ready. She took the envelope, folded it in two and wrapped it in the handkerchief from which she had taken a crumpled envelope of her own.

'There's seventy pounds in it,' he whispered. 'I hope it's enough.'

'Seventy!' she exclaimed, giving him her envelope. 'You did well.'

'When will you go?' He slipped her letter into his pocket.

'Tomorrow maybe.'

'Does your mother know?'

'She knows I'm going – that's all. It's better that way.'

'I suppose so,' he said doubtfully.

'I heard about lunch,' Mary said. 'I'm sorry.'

'I'm sorry too. I'll miss . . . talking and all.' He stopped in confusion and felt himself blush.

'I'll have to go now. I'd better say goodbye – just in case.'

'We'll meet again, won't we?'

'I'd like us to,' she said simply. 'Say a prayer for me, please.'

'I'll always pray for you, he said.

'I'll write.' She smiled and let her hand rest momentarily on his. 'Goodbye, Hugh.' She fashioned the words with her lips rather than spoke them.

He watched as she walked away from him, then looked at his hand where she had touched it and a smile softened his face.

She felt a loathing for herself. She could admire Hugh for his kindness and his honesty. But what was there in her that he could admire, that would not be a falsehood and a deception? If she liked him, and she did, if she felt drawn to him, and she thought she might, the only good thing she could do for him was not to keep in touch with him, in spite of her promise, not to let him know where she was. Maybe when she had remade herself, when she could look in a mirror and not feel ashamed, when she could say her prayers again with a good conscience.

She buried the kitten in the garden and shut herself in her room. She didn't lock the door. She didn't want to give her father the satisfaction of breaking it down, of being able to say that – somehow – he was the one to have been wronged again. He was adept at turning the tables like that, at making you feel guilty or responsible for things he did.

She heard him pass down the corridor and knew he'd be

back as soon as he discovered her absence. When he came he wrenched at the door so violently that it shot open and he stumbled in. He had expected resistance and had put more force behind his entr · than was necessary.

As always, after doing wrong, he looked apologetic. There was that expression that said he was sorry, but that it wasn't his fault. It used to work with her, once. Now it just filled her with anger. It was so dishonest. He never accepted responsibility for anything.

He stood looking at her and she looked back at him. For a long moment there was silence and then she heard herself say, 'I suppose you've come to drown me now.' There was no inflexion in the words, no emotion. They just detached themselves from her like a breath exhaled in the frozen waste that floats away in a glitter of frost. He winced, then shook his head and withdrew as silently as he came.

She heard him pacing about and knew that he hadn't finished with her yet. She no longer feared what he might do to her. She loathed it and was disgusted by it, but she was not afraid.

The pacing stopped and the door opened. 'I could have got you a dozen kittens any time,' he said with dry-lipped passion, 'or anything you wanted.'

She looked at him in silence.

'Tell me what you need,' he said. 'And I'll get it for you. All you have to do is tell me.'

'I just need to be left alone.' She knew it was the one answer he didn't want to hear, that he couldn't cope with.

'You know I'd do anything for you –' he began.

'Except leave me alone,' she snapped. She was determined to expose his self-deception and wanted to be sure he understood that there would be no more concessions on her part. Whatever he got from her from now on would have to be got by force or it wouldn't be got at all.

'Don't be unreasonable.' His speech became more passionate as he went on. 'You and I belong together always. It's like being – it's the same as being . . . married.'

'You are married,' she said coldly, 'but not to me. It's time you remembered that.'

'I'm not talking about that kind of marriage. I'm not talking about legal contracts and agreements about property. I'm not talking about families and children. All that's a distraction to hide the fact that there's nothing else there. What I'm talking about is two people – you and me – being together, because they need to be together. It's impossible for them to live apart. That's what I mean by married – blood calling to blood and soul to soul. You felt this once. I know you did. I feel it all the time. You still feel it – if only you'd listen. You say that if I loved you I'd let you alone. But I love you and I can't.'

He looked at her, his face and eyes full of mad conviction. 'I know you're confused. I know you don't feel able to make a decision, but I'm asking you to think about it. You're upset about what happened. You must forget that. I'm not a violent man. I'm not an unfeeling man – you ought to know that. All I want is that you should love me and rely on me and be with me always because how could I be contented anywhere if you were gone?'

He shivered, as if he were unbearably cold, all the time looking at her with those burning, dry-rimmed eyes. She sat, numb, and could say nothing.

'I'm going now. You asked me to leave you alone and I will. We'll talk again tomorrow. You'll be feeling better then. I want to see you happy – enjoying life. That's the way you and I should be. That's the way we will be.' He smiled a tortured, sickly smile and withdrew from the room.

She sat for a long time with her head in her hands, unable to think or to feel. A weariness that had nothing to do with tiredness or lack of sleep settled on her shoulders.

He stopped his pacing and began to undress. When he was naked he stared at himself in the glass. His body was sadly fallen away from what it had been on that summer day long ago. His hair was sparse now, and thinning; it lay subdued and inert on his crown. The skin of his face was wrinkled and liverish. The downturn of his mouth marked disillusion and blasted hopes. Yet, inside, he was the same. He was still as eager, still as diffident, still as easily discouraged and hurt – more easily, because the blood thinned with age and was less readily stanched.

He looked with disgust at the bloated body in the mirror and turned away. A thousand times before morning, temptation would come and he would have to restrain himself, if he were able to restrain himself. He sat on the cold bed and thought of her, warm, pliant, just a few steps down the corridor. He pushed back the bedclothes and got in. Turning off the light, he lay there in the darkness with his thoughts.

His sleep – such as it was – was troubled and broken. There were dreams, so vivid that it was easy to confuse them with reality. She was always in the dream or some-one like her. He couldn't be sure whether it was she or not, because her face was averted. Once, when he caught her shoulders and spun her round, he was shocked to find that she had no face at all. In the dream she was always moving away from him, floating out of his grasp like thistledown. When he called to her, her receding figure became smaller, more tenuous and more distant, until he had to screw up his face and shield his eyes with his hand to see her at all.

Mrs Ennis knocked on the door of Mary's old room before going in. Mary was sitting at the dressing table, writing in her diary. She looked up in alarm, closed the book and drew a scarf over it. Seeing that it was only her mother, she smiled.

'I was hoping you might have some news.'

'Everything's arranged,' Mary told her.

'When will you go?' Mrs Ennis closed the door and sat down. It would be an ease to her mind to have Mary safely out of the house.

'Maybe tomorrow.'

'I've been thinking about what you should do —'

'No.' Mary was emphatic. 'You must leave all that to me. I don't want him ever to be able to trace anything back to you. I'll make my own plans.'

'As long as you have a plan, girl. I don't want anything to go wrong.'

'Nothing will go wrong.'

'Won't you let me know that you're all right.'

'I'll ring.'

'Is that wise? What if he gets the call?'

'I've thought of that. I'll wait to see who answers before speaking. If he's the one, I'll hang up.'

'But then I won't know whether it's you or just a

wrong number.'

'I'll ring again immediately after. I'll let it ring three times and then hang up. You'll know, at least, that it was me and that I'm all right. I'll ring every day after that until I get you. How about you? What'll you do?'

Mrs Ennis shrugged philosophically. 'Carry on, girl, as I've always carried on – just go on living. At my age you don't expect very much. You'd be foolish to expect anything, because you'd only be disappointed.'

She blew her nose into a paper handkerchief and sniffed a determined sniff. She could see that her melancholy was affecting Mary. She watched her sitting in silence, looking down at the familiar carpet of her bedroom. She remembered Mary asking as a child what kind of flowers they were. They looked vaguely like roses, but when she had examined the roses in the garden, she had seen that they weren't really roses at all. Mary had come in, disillusioned, and announced that she didn't like the carpet any more. For a while she had pestered them to get a new one. Then she had forgotten all about it. She wondered if she was remembering it now.

'We never got the carpet for you, either,' she said, while Mary looked at her blankly. 'We never got anything for you, really.'

Perhaps if their relationship had been different, they would not be facing each other as they were now, on the brink of a parting, beyond which neither of them could see clearly.

'What will you take with you?' she asked.

'Just what I'll be wearing and a few things in a shoulder bag.'

To her mother in her sombre mood the words were

elegiac, carrying a significance beyond their intended meaning. Mary would be leaving home – perhaps for ever – and there was nothing of value for her to take with her. She would travel light. She would travel empty. Roots and support would have to come from elsewhere.

'But you can't walk off like that, as if you were just going out to buy a newspaper.'

'That's exactly the way I'll have to go,' Mary said, 'if I want to escape notice.'

'You'll need money.'

'I have some money. Don't ask how I got it. It's best you don't know.'

'I could open an account for you.'

'No,' Mary said vehemently. 'You mustn't. He'd find out and then you'd be the one to suffer.' She looked at her mother earnestly. 'I want you to know that I'm sorry for not being what I should have been.' She suddenly burst into tears. 'I'm sorry for not being the kind of daughter you'd like to have had.'

Mrs Ennis laid her hand on Mary's arm. 'Don't, child,' she said. 'I haven't been the right kind of mother, either. If I'd been different, we'd have had none of this. Don't blame yourself. It's all been said now and settled between us and you're never again to feel bad about it. If' – she stopped to wipe her eyes and keep down the surge of feeling that rose in her – 'if you can forgive me, I can forgive you.' What she did not add was that she could never – would never – forgive herself. She had been full of self-righteousness, seeing everyone's fault but her own. She had been so complacent about her virtue. Her journey to Lourdes had been typical. Her place was at home and she had left it just when her daughter had needed her most.

Mary clasped her hand over her mother's and they sat there for some time in silence.

Presently Mrs Ennis stood up, and leaning over the dark head, kissed her daughter's hair – a gesture she had not made since Mary's early childhood. 'I'll have to go now,' she said. 'Is everything all right between us?'

She was reassured by the way Mary lifted her head and smiled. It was a tentative smile, but it was as much as she could reasonably expect. This new-found relationship would take time to grow and become natural between them.

'Came at you with a hammer, did he?' Mr O'Brien said. 'Oh, a violent man, all right. I'll tell you a story about that fellow. One night, maybe twenty-five years ago, a crowd of us were in a pub when a chap called Jem Duffy took it into his head to tell a yarn about this wild young one from Maiden Lane – a rough area in those days, you understand?

'Before he could finish, your man Ennis jumped up and told him to apologise or he'd break his mouth. Jem just laughed. Ennis lifted a bottle and brought it down full belt on his head. Duffy fell like a poleaxed pig, with blood spouting from his ear and a cut as big as an open pocket in his scalp. Then Ennis grabbed him by the hair and kept smashing his skull against the counter. It happened so quickly that he had the poor fellow near beaten to death before any of us had the presence of mind to try and stop him. I was paralysed. I never saw anything so violent in my life.

'When we did manage to drag him off, Duffy was in a

bad way. His head was like a basin of mince. The poor fellow was never the same again. They said there was brain damage. His speech was slurred. He had the most ferocious headaches. A couple of months after, he had a bleeding from one eye and lost the sight of it. Worst of all, he changed from being a bit of a card and a tough sort of bullyboy into a nervous, timid kind of fellow that was always hearing noises in his head like a tap dripping, and looking over his shoulder in the dark for fear of God-knows-what.'

'Did your man go to jail?' Hugh asked.

'Suspended sentence. Duffy was vague about things. Contradicted himself under cross-examination, and – God forgive us all – no witnesses came forward. Nobody wanted to be involved. So you had the usual Irish thing: everybody was looking the other way or out having a slash at the time.'

SEVENTEEN

The day had begun so promisingly with a clear sky and crisp, frosty air. Mary, wearing a secret smile that glowed like an internal fire, hummed about the house. She and her mother had gone about their ordinary routine, tidying, cleaning, preparing vegetables. Mary's bag was packed and ready – a slack, lightly filled bag that would draw no attention. It carried her toilet things, a few changes of underwear, a couple of pairs of jeans, a sweater and a wool dress. These would have to do until she got a job and could buy what she needed.

They said little; a smile, a hand laid lightly on shoulder or arm, was enough to bind them closer than words had ever done. Frequent glances at the clock were the only signs of tension.

At noon they sat down at the kitchen table and sipped mugs of coffee. In the silence that surrounded them her mother was aware of her own sniffing. She blew her nose and shook her head vigorously.

Mary laid her hand on hers. 'I must go,' she whispered.

Mrs Ennis looked at the clock. 'Don't forget – ' she began.

Mary put her finger to her lips. 'Ssh!' she said. 'We've gone through all that. You'll be hearing from me.'

They kissed lip to cheek, then she was gone. Mrs Ennis blessed herself, crossed to the sink and began to peel the potatoes. When she had finished she turned to contemplate the photograph of Mary in her confirmation dress that stood in its gilt frame on the mantelpiece.

What had gone wrong? She should at that very moment be driving through unfamiliar towns, dreaming of strange streets that would soon be her streets, her place, tasting the freedom of being her own person. She still didn't understand how he had come to be there. She knew nothing, because she had not been allowed to talk to her mother.

There had been people waiting outside O'Leary's, women with shopping bags resting on the pavement, a young mother and child with a suitcase, embarking on a holiday. The little boy had a tight grip on his mother's hand and with the other was pointing down the street. The bus was coming – just an ordinary bus, dented, mud-caked – elbowing its way through the traffic. Her heart was racing. The bus was pulling into the pavement. All she had to do was get aboard.

She was stooping to hoist her shoulder bag when she was caught roughly by the arm, swung round and pushed in a running trot in the other direction. She was so busy trying to hold her balance that they had gone fifty yards and were out of the Square and the Main Street before she could make any effective protest.

'Where did you think you were going?' He slowed to a walk but still held her in that wrestler's grip.

In the distance she heard the huge diesel revving up. She struggled to break loose. Behind her, the bus eased itself into power. There was no sound in town at that moment but the throb of its engine carrying away her hopes.

She could have cried out for help. Why hadn't she? She'd been asking herself that question ever since. The first thing – the stupid thing – was that she didn't think of it. She was so upset, so overwhelmed, that she never thought of it. Even if she had, what difference would it have made? Who would have taken her seriously, with him smiling there beside her that bland, all-things-to-all-men smile? Some silly domestic quarrel, they would have guessed. You know what teenagers are like these days.

When they got home he rushed her upstairs and into his bedroom. He locked the door and put the key in his pocket. 'So, you were going away and leaving me?' he said, angry and reproachful.

She sat on the small bed and stared at the floor and said nothing.

He picked up her shoulder bag and tumbled out the contents on the floor. He opened her purse, took out the bundle of notes and counted them. 'Where did you get seventy pounds? Did she give it to you?'

'No,' she said. 'She knows nothing about . . . anything.'

'Is that a fact?' he gibed, pocketing the money. 'Where did you get it?'

'I sold the watch.' She might as well have struck him.

'You didn't! You wouldn't!' He seized her wrist to look. He rooted through her purse. When he couldn't find it, he unlocked the door and let himself out, locking it again behind him. She heard him go down the corridor and into her room. She heard him banging about there for a long time and then coming back.

'You sold the watch!' he said, in what sounded like genuine anguish. 'She put you up to this, didn't she? She planned everything.'

Suddenly he went berserk and attacked the bed, pummelling it with his fists, cursing it and her. Then he threw pillows and blankets to the four corners of the room. She sat in terror, not daring to make a sound. Next he opened the door and heaved the mattress out, crying, 'It's finished. It's over.' He dragged the heavy base after it, then lifted the headboard away from the wall and hurled it out too. 'We'll begin again, you and I,' he said. 'Things will be better with us.'

'Better for whom?' she challenged.

'This is your place now.' He ignored her protest. 'You'll stay here and do what I say. I'm locking the door until you can be trusted.'

'You may lock me up for the rest of my life, then,' she said.

'It's up to you,' he said. He went out and she heard him manhandling the bed down the stairs, thumping and bumping for what seemed like hours.

When he came back after lunch on Saturday, Hugh was surprised to find the supermarket closed and the checkout girls and a little group of women standing outside. He tried the door and found it was locked. He ran up the broad steps to the hall door and rang the bell. Below, the women whispered and glanced at their watches.

'Is he opening or what?' one of them shouted.

Hugh shrugged his shoulders and pressed the bell again. He could hear the sound expanding to fill the hollowness of the hallway.

'Well, I can't wait any longer,' a woman said.

He watched them drift off, then the hall door opened and Ennis came out.

'What the devil do you want?' His face was pale, his eyes bloodshot.

'The supermarket is locked. You've already lost some customers.'

'To hell with them,' Ennis shouted. 'Let it stay locked.'

'What do you want me to do? Will I open now or not?'

'I'll tell you what I want you to do. I want you to get to hell out of here and never come back. You're fired, boy.'

'You can't fire me without a reason,' Hugh protested.

'Any reasons I have I'll give to the guards,' Ennis said darkly. 'You'll be hearing from them soon enough.'

What did he mean? What was he accusing him of? 'I'd like to see Mrs Ennis,' he demanded.

'Maybe you would, but you're not going to.' Ennis turned and went in.

Hugh pressed the bell again. The door opened and Ennis shouted, 'Didn't I tell you to fuck off?'

'I'd like a word with Mary.' Hugh's voice trembled, but not from fear.

'She's gone,' Ennis said with a crooked smile. 'I thought you'd be the first to know. Wasn't it careless of her not to tell you!'

Hugh turned and went down the steps. There was enough in the man's expression and tone to alarm him.

Something had gone wrong.

He cycled away in a despondent mood. There was only one way of finding out what had happened. He would have to contact Mrs Ennis. He was passing the church when he saw the empty phone box. He dialled the Ennis number. Presently the receiver was lifted and he heard the voice of Ennis – very cautious and tentative – say, 'Yes?'

Disguising his voice, Hugh asked for Mrs Ennis.

'She's not here,' Ennis said gruffly and hung up.

The woman was contemptible, he told himself scornfully. She couldn't be relied on even to protect the interests of her daughter. He had found her blubbering in the kitchen when he came in early to lunch. She had made a great show of turning her back while she blew her nose and dried her eyes. He noticed she was hiding something in her hand. He recognised it by its little gilt frame as a photograph of Mary, taken at the time of her confirmation.

'Where is she?'

She hesitated, her liar's face and panic-ridden tone shouting a different message to the one her mouth was mumbling. 'In her room, I think.'

He ran upstairs, calling Mary, then raced down again. 'Where's she gone?'

She said nothing, but involuntarily her eyes went to the clock. Almost five minutes to one.

'The bus!' he shouted.

'No!' she screamed, running to the door to bar his exit. 'Let her go.'

'Out of my way.' He pushed her aside.

'For God's sake, let her go,' she pleaded. 'What's to

be the end of this if you don't?'

But he was already on his way, slamming the door behind him. He hurried towards the Square. He saw her dark head lurking in a doorway. He broke into a lope that made people turn and stare. He saw the bus butting its way to the stop. He heard the screech of the doors. She was stooping to pick up her shoulder bag.

With a lunge, he grabbed her arm and forced her away. When he had steered her into the calm of Spurgeon Street, he dropped into a more conventional pace and warned, 'One false move and I'll tell that fellow – everything. I mean everything.' He squeezed her arm and felt her wince. 'Smile, damn you, smile – and don't have people staring at us.'

At home he hurried her up to his bedroom. It was that damned witch downstairs who had poisoned the girl's ear. He glared at the bed. It looked so full of the promise of warmth and intimacy. The thing was a sick lie. It was a grave in which all his dreams had been buried. He started to pound it as if it were living flesh, shouting at it, getting angrier as it absorbed his attack in its inert, maddening way. He pulled it out and heaved it down the stairs. He would burn it before her eyes and put an end, once and for all, to the pretence that something called a marriage existed between them.

He knew she was watching from the kitchen as he dragged it down the garden. With an axe he smashed the base and headboard. He poured paraffin over the lot, then went indoors and caught his wife by the arm. 'Out!' he ordered. 'There's something I want you to see.'

With a little crooked smile and a shrug that infuriated him, she went out. He pushed her into the garden seat, drew a box of matches from his pocket, struck a fistful and threw them at the heaped pile of bedding.

'There!' he shouted, as flame enveloped the bed and whooshed upwards with a roar. 'That's the end of you and me. Finished! Done! For ever!'

He watched the flames leap and glide, the padding blacken and curl, and great eddies of smoke corkscrew upwards and hang darkly over the garden. He could feel his venom spewing out in those sombre flames. He felt light-headed with the release of tension. He raised his voice in a wordless whoop, going back to emotions that pre-dated language, as intense and instinctive as the cry of an animal.

It was some time before he recalled her presence there, stiff and unmoving, with an expression on her face that was blank, frozen. He turned away until the crunch of her feet across the frosted grass told him she had gone indoors.

Mary had spent the afternoon pacing and looking out the window. In the garden he came and went in violent surges and ebbings, drowning the place with his presence and then leaving it drained. Over on the rough concrete, where he burned rubbish, he had assembled a strange pile. All afternoon she'd watched him – headboard, base, that huge spring mattress with the dips in the middle – one deep, one shallow – lying out on the frosty grass. So close together those depressions – one his, one hers – the history of twenty-two years. But a false history.

She had heard the thud of the axe and ran to look. She saw the wood burst apart. He kept swinging at it long after it had collapsed into matchwood. In the same way he battered the base and then attacked the mattress until the springs broke through. She watched him sprinkle paraffin over the pieces he had heaped together in a pyramid and then go indoors. When he came out he was pushing her mother, who made no resistance and no sound.

She had rattled her fists on the window and called out. She had tried to open the casement to put her head out but it was jammed. There was nothing she could do but beat on the pane and shout. He heard her, because he looked up, but it didn't deter him. He continued to push her mother down the garden. Why didn't she struggle? Why didn't she shout?

He pushed her into the seat under the apple tree. He took a box of matches from his pocket, struck several and threw them at the pyramid, which burst into a high, transparent flame. He pranced round it with a garden fork, tossing up pieces of broken bed that fell, scattering sparks. The higher the flame, the thicker the smoke, the more excited he grew. She could hear him shouting at her mother.

She watched her sitting there, with her head tilted to take in the dark cloud that hung over the garden and the house. By now the wood had caught fire and burned with a deeper glow, pulsing like a living thing. Eventually, except for pale coils, there was no trace of bed or mattress left and everything was reduced to a tight mass that collapsed in on itself in a white incandescence, along which blue flames darted and flickered.

Her mother stood up and went in stiffly, like someone whose joints were turning rheumaticky. She neither looked at him nor spoke. When she had gone indoors, he sat down on the seat and remained there, staring at the fire.

EIGHTEEN

Hugh rode through busy streets until he found himself passing the supermarket and house again. He saw smoke rising over the roof and stopped to watch. The house was on fire.

He leaped off the bicycle, ran up the steps and leaned on the bell. There was no answer. He shouted, but still there was no response. The dark coils rose steadily and massed overhead. A few people had gathered and were looking up at the cloud overhanging the house.

'Fire!' he shouted. 'Somebody ring for the fire brigade.'

People looked at him curiously and moved back but nobody made any attempt to find a phone.

He remounted, raced to the church and rang the emergency number that was posted up in the box. 'There's a fire at Ennis's on the Killawley Road,' he shouted. 'It looks bad.'

'The brigade is out,' a voice said. 'I'll try to contact them.'

Hugh hung up, then lifted the receiver again and dialled

the Garda barracks. He reported the fire and cycled back to observe the house from the shelter of a butcher's awning. The dark pall had drifted off to the north-east. Thin ringlets of grey curled upwards over the roof and broke into diffuse strands. The smoke seemed to be coming from somewhere at the back rather than from the house.

He had been there a few minutes when a Garda car drew up. Two uniformed men got out. Their eyes were drawn to the roof and the pale smoke-plume. They ran up the steps. One pressed on the bell, while the other tried to peer through the central panel of frosted glass. He watched them awhile, then mounted and cycled towards them. The door opened as he was passing and Ennis came out. Their eyes met for an instant.

Now was the time to ring Mrs Ennis, while her husband was still on the doorstep. The kiosk at the church was occupied. Two giggling girls took turns in using the receiver and seemed set to continue for the afternoon. He waited impatiently before tapping on the glass. They looked at him, nudged each other, shrugged and resumed their conversation.

He set off towards his lodgings in Mill Street. There was a pay-phone in the hall. He could call her from there. A word with her would be enough to tell him what he wanted to know.

He would have to get her out of there before the night passed. That damned Dolan was set on making a nuisance of himself. He had recognised him on the phone. He was bound to ring again. Sacking him had been a mistake. All he had done was to alert the fellow and make him suspicious. It would have been simpler to have given him the key and kept him occupied in the supermarket. The wisdom of this was proved when Sergeant Evans and Garda Cloonan arrived with their policemen's curiosity. Of course, it had been Dolan who had brought them down on him. But it was likely that the fool had overreached himself. He had been able to point him out to the sergeant as he cycled away. It had made it possible to blame him for raising a false alarm and to send the sergeant in pursuit to his digs.

'Spite, sergeant,' he had told him. 'He has it in for me because I fired him today.'

'Why did you fire him?' the sergeant asked.

'It's a . . . delicate matter.' Ennis lowered his voice. 'I found out this morning that he was planning to run away with my daughter Mary. She's an innocent, foolish girl – sixteen years old – and easily led. When I found out, I gave him his cards. Then there was the matter of the till.'

'You caught him dipping his fingers in?'

'Not exactly caught. I've been missing small sums over a period. I've had my suspicions, but I couldn't prove anything. When I brought Mary back from the bus today, she had seventy pounds on her – that's about the sum total of what's been missing over the past few weeks. She said she got it from Dolan.'

'She was actually running away and you stopped her?'
'Yes.'

'Did you mention your daughter's leaving to him?' the sergeant asked.

'I pretended she had gone – just to keep him guessing.'

'You hadn't words about it – an argument, or anything like that?'

'No.'

'You didn't accuse him of making free with the till?'

'No. I just fired him.'

'Good,' the sergeant said. 'Wise. It's better not to translate suspicions into accusations in the heat of the moment. Now I'd like a word with your good lady, if I may, and after that, with your daughter.'

'They're upset at the moment,' Ennis said. 'Would it be all right to leave it till later?'

'Very well, but if you wish to pursue a charge against Dolan, I'll have to interview them.'

There were complications inherent in this, which Ennis was quick to see.

'I'm not sure if I want to press charges against anyone,' he said. 'I'd have to think very carefully before I could allow my little girl and her mother to be dragged through the courts, and private matters laid open like that. All I'm saying is that Dolan may well have made a nuisance of himself and committed an offence by pretending there was a dangerous fire when there wasn't.'

The sergeant nodded sagely. 'I'll talk to him first, and then we'll see.'

Ennis watched them drive off before going indoors thoughtfully. He had already decided to take Mary away. Now he would have to get her out of the house before the sergeant returned to interview her. There was just one problem. He'd need money and the bank wouldn't open again until Monday. He'd have to find some place to hide her away, where she would be safe and inaccessible over the weekend.

* * *

When he turned into Mill Street, Hugh was surprised to see the squad car standing at the door and Mrs O'Brien in conversation with two guards.

'Here he is now,' he heard her say as he drew up. She looked at him a little strangely before going inside. It was clear that she was wondering what he was doing, cycling about on a busy Saturday afternoon.

'Are you Hugh Dolan?' Sergeant Evans asked.

'That's right, sergeant,' he said.

'Did you ring the barracks a while back?'

'Yes, I did.'

'You were the one who reported a fire at Ennis's?'

'The fire brigade was out, so I rang the barracks. Did I do something wrong?'

'It has been said that your call was malicious, designed to cause embarrassment to Mr Ennis. What have you to say to that?'

'Why should I do a thing like that?' Hugh asked. 'There was a fire, wasn't there? It looked bad too.'

'Mr Ennis says he was only burning rubbish.'

'I didn't know that. I thought the house was on fire and I reported it.'

'And it had nothing at all to do with the fact that you were sacked?'

'Nothing.'

'Do you mind telling us why you were dismissed?'

'I don't know. You'll have to ask Mr Ennis. All I know is that when I went back after lunch the supermarket was closed. When I went looking for the key, he came out and fired me.'

'And you walked off without finding out why? That doesn't make sense.'

'It would if you knew the man you were dealing with.'

'It would make better sense if you already knew why you were being sacked. It was put to me that you did know. What have you to say to that?'

'I didn't and don't,' Hugh said flatly.

'Do you know Mary Ennis?'

'Yes, I do.'

'Know her well, I dare say? Fancy her a bit, maybe?'

'She's a nice girl,' Hugh said guardedly.

'Too nice a girl to be pestered and pressurised,' Garda Cloonan said.

'I don't know what you mean.' He wondered what lies Ennis had told them.

'What was the relationship between you and Mary Ennis?' the sergeant asked.

'We were friends,' Hugh said. 'I gave her a kitten once. He didn't tell you about that, I'd swear.'

'I put it to you,' the sergeant said, 'that you were no friend of this girl, that you took advantage of her.'

'Is that what he said?' Hugh asked angrily. 'If he did, he's a liar. Why don't you ask Mary herself? She'll tell you the truth.'

'You know where she is, then?' the sergeant asked.

'No. Isn't she at home?'

'You deny, then, that you conspired with her to "borrow" a sum of money from the till and run away together?'

'I certainly do,' Hugh said.

'I'd like to believe you,' the sergeant smiled. 'But there's one thing bothering me. For a man who's been fired, you seem greatly unconcerned. I find that hard to understand. But it would be easy to understand if you actually wanted to be fired, if you had already made up your mind to leave with Miss Ennis. What would you say to that?'

'If I was supposed to be away with Mary, why am I here talking to you and not somewhere else?' Hugh said with uncharacteristic sarcasm.

'You planned to follow her later,' the sergeant said.

'Am I being accused of committing a crime, or what?' Hugh asked.

'You're the first to mention a crime,' the sergeant said.

'No, I'm not,' Hugh reminded him. 'You mentioned taking money. Is that what I'm being accused of?'

'You were accused of nothing. You were merely invited to deny certain suggestions.'

Hugh was confused. Though he knew he had done nothing wrong, the suggestion that he might have done – especially when it was made by a Garda sergeant in full uniform – was enough to give a shifty look to his eye and bring a flush to his cheeks. 'I swear to God I've done nothing wrong.'

'Never swear unless you have to,' the sergeant advised. 'This is not a sworn inquiry. It's merely a preliminary investigation. So, no swearing. Now, tell the truth. Did you know that Mary Ennis planned to leave home?'

'I – may have,' Hugh said warily.

'Did you or didn't you?'

'I did. Is there anything wrong with that?'

'Did you persuade or encourage her to go?'

'No. I did not.'

'There would,' Sergeant Evans said delicately, 'be contrary opinions on that.'

'They're not true,' Hugh replied angrily.

'Let's hear the truth, then,' the sergeant invited. 'Tell us what you know of Mary Ennis and her plans to leave home.'

As quietly and unsensationally as he could, Hugh told them of Mary's problems at home, as far as he understood them, of her wish to get away and start a new life somewhere else, and of how he had helped her by lending her seventy pounds of his own money. To simplify matters, he made no mention of the watch or his attempts to sell it. He insisted that he had never planned to accompany her or join her later. Nothing that either of them should be ashamed of had ever happened between them. By the time he had finished, he felt courage enough to ask where Mary was and if she was all right.

'She's at home and well,' Sergeant Evans said. 'Her father persuaded her to change her mind.'

Hugh's face was a book in which anyone who cared to look could read disappointment.

'The news doesn't please you?' the sergeant said, in a tone inviting confidence.

'It doesn't sound true. *Forced her* might be more like it. Mary was bent on getting away. She wouldn't have stayed willingly.'

'That would be your interpretation of things. On the other hand, she may have had second thoughts, at the last moment. There's all the difference in the world between planning something and actually carrying it out.'

'Maybe you should ask her what happened. She'll tell you why she wanted to go and what stopped her.'

'I intend to ask her. As for you, whether you'll be hearing from me again depends to a great extent on what Miss Ennis has to tell me and what her mother has to say. Meanwhile, I'll suspend judgement about the fire.'

'I reported the fire because I thought the house was in danger,' Dolan maintained stubbornly.

'For the moment' – the sergeant drew on his gloves – 'we'll leave it at that. Please keep yourself available for questioning – and stay away from Miss Ennis and her family.'

NINETEEN

Mrs Ennis sat at the kitchen table with her head in her hands. Her silly sentimentality had ruined everything. If only she had had the good sense to behave normally, Mary would be safe by now.

What was she going to do? Burning the bed had been an act of lunacy; it was terrifying. She had watched the fire in fascination, wondering with a resigned dread what was to follow. She remembered hoping that the burning would be enough to satisfy his anger.

Before the night was out she might have to call the guards. Would it be possible to do it without going into all the details? Would it be enough to tell them that he had terrorised and beaten both of them? His burning of the bed could be used to show the irrationality of his behaviour.

But would the guards help her? And if they did, wouldn't they treat it as just another family quarrel, the kind of thing they were called in to arbitrate on every Saturday night in places like St Ivor's Terrace – the kind of thing that worked its way through the courts a few months later and rumbled through the pages of the local paper? Would that help Mary? Once the thing was set in motion, there was no telling where it would stop or how it could be contained. The fact was that it could not be contained.

The darkness of evening had fallen and she was still there, her problem unresolved. She was disturbed by the opening of the door and the snapping on of the light. She watched her husband, dressed for going out, take milk from the fridge and pour it into a glass, then cut and butter awkward slices of bread and arrange them on a plate.

'You can't keep her locked up like that,' she said.

'I don't intend to.' The reasonableness of his tone took her by surprise. 'As soon as she gives me her word that she won't attempt anything foolish she can have the run of the house.' He indicated the milk and the bread. 'I'm taking these up to her. She'll be all right until I come back.'

She looked at him suspiciously. What was he planning? 'When will that be?' she asked. There was something threatening in his agreeableness. He was most to be feared when he was like that.

'No need to play the dutiful wife and wait up for me.' The familiar note of sarcasm was back.

'You can't keep her locked up like that,' she protested again.

'You'd better speak to her, then. She seems to listen to you now.' The last was spoken by way of accusation.

She heard him go upstairs and come down again. Then she heard the front door slam and the car engine sharp and metallic in the frosty air. Where was he off to? What had he in mind? Obviously he intended to be late, or was that only another of his tricks to deceive and confuse her?

She went up the stairs and saw the key in the lock.

Scarcely trusting her eyes, she reached out and turned it. The door opened and there was Mary, dishevelled and tearful, the milk and bread untouched on the dressing table. She took her by the hand and together they tiptoed downstairs. What was he up to? What did it mean?

'He's planning to take me away. Did you know that?' Mary cried.

'You must get out of here before he comes back.' Mrs Ennis looked at the clock. It was a little after half six.

'He said he'd be late. He has to arrange something,' Mary told her.

'How did he forget the key? He may miss it and come back. Maybe he left it just to test us and will burst in any minute now.'

'What'll we do?' Mary wailed.

'If you hurry, you'll catch the seven o'clock bus. Run and get your things together. I'll make a few sandwiches. Hurry for God's sake!'

'But I've no money. He took it off me.'

Mrs Ennis found her purse, opened it and held out a bundle of notes. 'I wanted you to take this before. There's two hundred in it.'

Mary took the money gratefully and ran upstairs. When she came down again, her mother stuffed a parcel of sandwiches into her shoulder bag.

'When you get to the city, go straight to a hotel and take a room for the night. Get an early train for Dublin in the morning. You'll have most of the day left to find a place. If all fails, try a convent or a priest's house. They'll help you. You must go now. Out the back way – just in case. Wrap yourself up well.'

They clung together. Then she opened the back door and

Mary slipped out.

'I'll be praying for you,' her mother whispered, as she crossed the darkened yard to the alley. She heard the gate grate and grind. She bolted the door. It was still only ten to seven. Barely twenty minutes had passed since she had found the key in the lock.

She went upstairs and down the corridor to the room. She looked into the wardrobe. All his clothes were gone, except for two suits, which he hadn't worn for years. So it was true. He did intend to leave. He had already packed and loaded the car. There would be uproar when he came back.

She was about to leave the key in the lock when it occurred to her that it would help to delay discovery if she removed it. She took it with her downstairs and left it in the hallway near the front door. It was the sort of place where he might easily have dropped it as he put on his overcoat.

She watched the minute hand of the kitchen clock creep round to seven, and sat alert, straining for distant sounds, picking up the breathing and sighing of the house, the roof beams flexing and relaxing, the drumbeat of her heart. She walked into the hall to listen. A car approached, changed its pitch and receded. Much relieved she went back to the kitchen, made a cup of tea, and slipped two slices of bread into the toaster. She felt hungry and remembered that she hadn't eaten since morning. The popping of the toaster made her start.

Confidence crept into her with the tea. The bus would be well on its way by now. She saw Mary sitting there, her face reflected in the glass, that frown of anxiety relaxed a little.

At the first ring of the telephone she jumped in confusion. She rushed to the hallway as it rang again. She was standing beside it when it rang a third time. She reached out her hand and hesitated – trying to remember her instructions. It rang a fourth time and went dead. She looked at her watch. It was only seven thirty. Patience was what she needed. It would be an hour yet before she could reasonably expect a call from Mary. She was turning to go when the phone rang again.

'Hello,' she said, in a voice that was hesitant and not a little fearful.

'Hello.' A voice came faint over the line. 'Could I speak to Mrs Ennis?'

'Speaking,' she said. 'Is that Hugh?'

'Yes. I was wondering if you had any news of Mary? She told me she might be . . . going away in the afternoon.'

'Not in the afternoon,' she said carefully. 'She went at seven.'

'Seven?'

'Yes. Why?'

'I just . . . wondered.' Dolan said. 'Could I come over to see you?'

'Is it about what happened today – that unpleasantness with my husband?'

'You heard about me being fired, then?'

'I didn't know that. Is that what you want to see me about?'

'Not exactly.' The voice was edgy in a way that worried her. 'May I ask if your husband is there now?'

'No,' she said, feeling that she understood the cause of his unease at last. 'He went out. He won't be back for hours. So come straight over.'

She washed the tea things and tidied them away. The sound of the doorbell made her start. Her nerves were jangled and on edge, her mind anticipating disaster. She opened the door and let Hugh into the hall. He refused to remove his overcoat. He was not at ease, looking nervously about him and lifting his head to listen. It was understandable, she felt, for him to be like that after a confrontation with her husband. He would be anxious to avoid another.

'Are you sure you won't come in and sit down?' she said.

'Can't, I'm afraid.' He pushed up the sleeve of his overcoat to look at his watch. 'I'm to meet a fellow who's giving me a lift home.'

'What's this about being fired?'

'Mr Ennis accused me of taking money. I never took a penny of anybody's money in my life.'

'Of course you didn't,' Mrs Ennis said. 'I'll talk to him. I'll see what I can do.'

'What I really came to ask,' he said hesitantly, 'was how Mary went off. Was it on the bus?'

'Yes – the seven bus.' She looked at him, her suspicions, fears, nightmares rushing to the surface. 'Why? Is there . . . something?'

'I don't know. I didn't see the bus. But I saw Mr Ennis around that time – in the car.'

'The car!' she said with relief. 'You gave me a fright. I thought . . . '

'I don't know whether I should say this – it's not easy to see at night and the glass was frosted. But I'm almost certain there was somebody with him.'

'It could be anybody,' she reasoned desperately.

'I thought it was Mary. They seemed to be arguing.'

'No, no' – she shook her head – 'it wasn't Mary. Mary was . . . Oh, God! What are we going to do?'

'Maybe I made a mistake,' he tried to console her. 'I couldn't be sure.'

It was Mary, all right. How clever he had been, anticipating what she would do. It might have been days – even weeks – before she found out. What could she do now that she had found out? To get some response from the guards she would have to tell them everything, and, even then, they might not believe her.

'Where did you see the car? Which way were they going?'

'That's the odd thing,' Hugh said. 'They were heading out the coast road. It doesn't go anywhere. It just doubles round Torc Head and comes back to town another way.'

'It goes past Gortnaheensha,' she said. It seemed to her in a flash that his strategy had been made plain. He would leave Mary in Gortnaheensha, come back to town, pretend to discover her 'escape' and take off in pursuit. Then he would collect her and disappear. As far as the world was concerned – as far as she was concerned – he would have gone in search of her. By the time the truth was discovered – if it ever was discovered – they would be far away. If she was right, he would return shortly.

'Gortnaheensha?' Hugh looked to her for explanation.

'My home place. It's that big Georgian house in the trees before you come to Torc Head. It's a retreat house, now, for the Patrician fathers. There's never anybody there this time of year. My husband has the key. He keeps an eye on the place for them.'

'Why would he bring her there?'

There was a limit to what she could tell Dolan. But she needed his help. 'To lock her up in the empty house,' she said. 'That'd be his idea of punishment for going off without his permission. He did it, once, to her brother Tom when he was a child.'

What was to be done? Whatever it was, it would have to be done quickly. He might very well be on his way back already. She turned to Hugh. 'What time did you say you were to meet that friend of yours?'

'I don't have to go home at all,' he said, 'if I could be of any use here. I'll send a message with Eugene. There's no problem about that.'

Mrs Ennis was grateful for the offer. 'You don't understand all this, of course. How could you! And there's no time to explain.'

'What would you like me to do?' Hugh was eager to help.

'Would you – would it be too much to ask you to go out to Gortnaheensha and have a look round? There's a key I could give you. If he does come back here – and he said he would – you'd be able to get in and find Mary – if she's there – and take her out before he went back.'

Hugh buttoned up his coat. 'I'll go by the digs and leave a message for Eugene on my way.'

Mrs Ennis handed him a key which she took from a drawer. 'The front door,' she said.

'Where'll I take her if I find her? Back here?'

'Oh, no!' she said. 'No! That wouldn't do at all.'

After giving the matter some thought, they decided that he would take her to the Dunraven Arms Hotel on the northern edge of town and book her in for the night. She would be safe there until her father cooled down. Dolan would ask her to ring home as soon as she got settled in. If she was not at Gortnaheensha, he was to ring immediately from the house.

When he had gone she sat around waiting for her husband's return – nervous, uneasy, alert to every sound. Time passed and she wondered if he would come at all. What if Dolan had been mistaken? There was still a chance that Mary had got away on the bus and was now beyond his reach.

When he did come, it was so silently that it startled her. The kitchen door opened and he looked in with that wide stare of his. There was an excited air about him that communicated itself to her immediately. He withdrew without a word being spoken and she heard him go upstairs. In a moment he was down again. The door burst open and he rushed in to confront her.

'I want that key.' He advanced on her with raised fist.

She cowered back from him. There was no need to pretend fear. She felt it deeply enough. 'There's a key in the hallway.'

'Get it.'

She went out and picked up the key where it lay close to the skirting board. He snatched it from her and ran up the stairs.

'You're too late,' she called, playing out her part of the charade. 'She's gone.'

The words halted his momentum for a second, then, with an oath, which seemed too authentic to be feigned, he took the rest of the stairs at a leap, raced down the corridor and opened the bedroom door.

'Where is she?' He advanced belligerently down the stairs.

'Gone,' she said, 'where you can't lay your filthy hands on her.'

'She hadn't any money.'

'I gave her some.'

'You bitch!' He caught her roughly and pushed her ahead of him up the stairs. With the back of his hand he struck her full in the face and sent her reeling across the bedroom floor. 'I'll find her,' he said, 'and when I do, I've some unfinished business to settle with you.' He spat in disgust and went out, locking the door behind him. She heard the hall door open and close. Then a car started up and shot off at speed.

She mopped her numbed mouth and wondered what, if anything, she had achieved. She was locked inside an empty house with no means of communication with Mary or Dolan. She still could not be certain whether her worst fears were well founded or not. The only thing she could be sure of was that her husband had come back as she had predicted.

A long time elapsed before she heard the phone ring downstairs. It rang once . . . twice . . . three times . . . and stopped.

TWENTY

She had been through so much that she felt exhausted. She was tempted to lay her head down and drift off for ever, but knew she mustn't let that happen. She would burrow deep inside herself, like the African fish that burrows into the mud when the river bed dries up, and survives there in clay hardened to stone until the rains come again to release it.

When he had stepped out of the alley and bundled her into the car, she couldn't even scream. Her mouth was dry with terror. How had he known that she'd come out that way? What if she'd gone out the front door instead? Had he been lying in wait for her all the time? He foresaw everything. He anticipated everything.

She remembered coming to Gortnaheensha as a child. She remembered cycling out by the bay in summer, with the sun skimming and bouncing like a flat stone over the water. The garden had been full of long foxgloves. She used fit her fingers into their purple thimbles.

The room she was in was the superior's room. There was

a prie-dieu with a green cushion facing a crucifix on the wall. There was the desk she was sitting at and a locker beside the bed, with the Child of Prague standing on it.

They had no sooner got inside than he rushed her upstairs, pulled off her jeans and took her, his trousers about his ankles and his shoes on his feet. He had hurt her so much, piercing her like iron, that she wanted to scream. But the more he hurt, the more determined she was not to show it.

He had gone off then, but he would be back. They were to stay there till Monday. He had taken out food from the supermarket to tide them over and brought it up while she crawled in under the blankets of the priest's bed and lay there pretending to be asleep.

She used to feel dirty afterwards, violated. Now she was learning to separate herself from what was happening. She had reason to feel dirty at the beginning. She had been part of it then. She wished she could turn the clock back and blot all that out.

He'd be returning soon. She knew his plans. 'We'll have more time later on,' he had said by way of apology. 'We'll take time over it. We'll have my girl back again. We'll entice that wild little lady out of her den – I haven't seen her around for a long time – and make such a night of it as we'll never forget.' His eyes had that wide, faraway look, the pupils dilated and dark, a little half-smile on his face, as he stared beyond her at whatever vision he saw there.

It was a brittle night with a fragile sliver of moon suspended overhead when Ennis left home and got into his car. He drove out the coast road, listening to the crunch of tyres on ice. It was a little after nine. He turned his mind to the night ahead and to the future. She would get over her withdrawn spell.

As he turned into the avenue the headlights, probing through columns of pine, caught the façade of Gortna-heensha and movement on the gravel in front. Someone was carrying a ladder towards the house. He stopped the car, switched off the lights and engine, and taking a torch from the glove compartment, got out and approached the house on foot. When he came to the oval sweep of gravel, he saw the ladder leaning against the wall under Mary's window on the first floor. Someone was beginning to climb.

He slipped from tree to tree until he was opposite the ladder, then stepped onto sliding gravel, which grated underfoot. It was no use trying to approach unheard over that treacherous surface. He waited until the figure was halfway up, then leaped forward, setting off minor explosions wherever he grounded his feet. He saw the figure turn in alarm, and snapped on the torch, catching Dolan's face full in the beam. Then he was on him, pulling him off the ladder, beating at him with the torch, punching him and tearing at his hair.

Hugh fought back like a mad thing, but a blow of the torch under his ear sent him reeling. In an instant Ennis had him down, with his knee on his neck. He twisted his hands and pinned them behind his back.

'What are you doing snooping around here?'

'Why have you locked her up? Let her out or I'll go to the guards.'

'I'll take you there myself,' Ennis threatened. 'Breaking and entering is a serious offence.'

'So is holding a person against her will.'

'Listen, you busybody,' Ennis shouted, 'you're butting in where you're not wanted. She doesn't care about you. You're no more to her than the dirt under her fingernails. She's promised. She belongs to someone else.'

'Who?' Hugh wanted to know.

'Let me spell it out for you.' Ennis kneed him in the ribs, punctuating what he said with blows. 'That – girl – is – married. Now – do you understand?'

'Lies!' Hugh yelled. 'Who's she married to?'

Something reckless in Ennis was throbbing again. 'Are you sure you want to know? Are you sure you're man enough to know?'

'Tell me.'

'She's married to me. She's mine.'

'You're out of your mind,' Hugh shouted. He struggled to free himself, but Ennis ground his face into the gravel.

'You know nothing about anything, do you?' he said. 'You've never heard of fathers and daughters liking each other so much, craving each other so much, hungry for each other so much, that they can't stay apart?'

'Stop! You bastard!'

'I'll tell you another thing. It was she who started it. It was she who came to me – burning and shameless and open, begging me to take her.'

'You rotten liar!' Hugh shouted. With a lunge and an up-ward thrust he freed himself and went staggering across the gravel.

'Ask her. Go on and ask her,' Ennis taunted, as Hugh swayed into the cover of the pine trees. Ennis ran indoors, and seizing a shotgun and some cartridges he had stowed there, he rushed out, raised the gun to his shoulder and fired twice. He ran across the gravel, loading as he went, aware of cries from the house behind him, and in front the snapping of dead wood. He fired at random, then stood and listened. The night was silent.

He loaded again and stepped cautiously between the trees. He came out by the gate and stood in the shelter of a pier to listen. From nearby came the cranking of a bicycle chain under strain. As he listened it grew fainter, falling away to a dry rasp and then to nothing at all. He crossed the avenue and combed down the other side for the best part of half an hour. There was no sign of Dolan. Either he had slipped through the fence into the wider plantation beyond, or he was on his way back into town. Ennis came round to the gravelled ellipse again and looked at the lighted window. The bastard must have been lurking about the street and followed them out there.

He stood by the ladder, looking up. He put his foot on the first rung and began to ascend. If he had a peep at her unobserved, he might be able to determine her state of mind and gauge what had happened. His head came over the sill and he saw the white net curtains above him. He stepped higher and stared into the room. Inside, staring anxiously out – scarcely six inches separating them – he met the pale face of his daughter. He watched in dismay as she screamed, then flew to the bed and covered her head in the blankets.

He climbed down, took the ladder and carried it into the hall. He locked the door behind him and went upstairs. With Dolan loose, they could not stay there – unless, by some stroke of luck, one of those shots had got him. It was comforting to think of him out in the plantation, his sightless eyes turned to the stars, and the frost already whitening his eyebrows.

On the other hand, if that was his bicycle he had heard cranking back into town, what then? But what could the bastard do? He could hardly make contact with her, locked up as she was, and the guards were not likely to give him much hearing, unless he was able to convince them with something like a gunshot wound. Even then it would be Dolan's word against his. A man had a right to protect his daughter from a ruffian. And when that ruffian had found her hiding place and was caught in the act of breaking in, wasn't it understandable for a father to sound off a couple of shots at him by way of warning? And if the girl was to support Dolan against him, wasn't that understandable too? Sergeant Evans was a father himself and a reasonable man. He would not be likely to give Dolan too much credence.

A new idea struck him. Why shouldn't he phone the barracks himself? He could say that he had been making a routine check, found someone breaking in and had fired a couple of shots to scare the intruder. Then, if Dolan were foolhardy enough to complain, he might very well be held for questioning. Even if the guards did take his story seriously, it would be simple to deny that Mary had ever been there and refer them to his wife, who had sent her off – for a holiday. All he had to do was to get in with his story before Dolan. He would have to be careful, though, to discourage the guards from coming out to examine the house.

He turned to go downstairs to ring them, but the noise of glass breaking sent him racing upwards instead.

He put the key into the lock and wrenched the door open. Mary stood on a chair, sobbing and beating with her shoe at splinters of glass around the rim of a hole in the windowpane. He caught her and bundled her onto the bed, where she screamed and beat at him ineffectually.

'Don't touch me. Leave me alone.'

''Twas only that fellow snooping around. I soon put the run on him.'

'You fired at him. You could have killed him.'

'What harm if he's lying out there, that damned face of his blasted with shot! He's nothing to us.'

'He's my friend,' she cried. 'The only friend I have.'

'Only?' he shouted. 'What do you mean *only*? Haven't I always been your friend? What do you want with anyone else when you've me? I'm all you'll ever need. I'd wipe that fellow off the face of the earth if I thought he could give you anything I couldn't. Can't you see I'm jealous of him, dammit? Here I am, laying myself bare to you like this, admitting things I'd be slow to admit to myself. And why am I doing it? Because I can't do without you, that's why; because I couldn't live two minutes if you were gone. I wouldn't want to live. There'd be nothing to live for. You talk to me about friends. *Friend* is a poor word for the feelings I have for you.'

'You could have been my father. To want to be anything else is wrong.' Mary's tone was hard.

'There's no right or wrong when the blood calls. There's only a need that must be satisfied. You feel it too. I know you do. It was there in the beginning. Your instinct told you that there could be love,' he ranted.

'It was incest. Why don't you call it by its right name?'

'What's a name like that, only a false label thought up by people for something they're afraid of? What happened between you and me was good.'

'It was incest. From the beginning. Now it's rape as well. You talk about love. What has love to do with rape? What has love to do with locking me up like this? What has love to do with terrorising me? What has love to do with trying to kill the only friend I have? I hate you.'

'Don't say that.' He caught her roughly by the shoulders and shook her, his hands tightening about her and encompassing her neck. He pounded her head against the pillows in rhythm with the words, beating and shaking and bringing his strong fingers together. 'It's not true. Say it isn't true. Say it, damn you! Say it.'

He pressed his thumbs into her throat, intent on forcing the words out of her. She struggled and plunged desperately, trying to rid herself of those steely fingers that were slowly choking her. The more she struggled, the more his grip tightened, held, locked. She felt her chest swell and expand to bursting point. Her head throbbed. Her ears rang. She felt faint. After one final reflexive plunge her resistance weakened to an ineffectual fluttering and her body went limp. When he became aware of it, it seemed to him just another trick of hers. He continued to shake her and shout abuse, then flung her from him and heard her head hit the wall with a sound no larger than the cracking of an eggshell.

Immediately he was contrite. He hadn't meant to hurt her. She was lying oddly, her head at a strange angle to her body. 'Don't do that to me.' He was suddenly afraid. 'Don't pretend like that.' He lifted her head into a more natural position and stooped to kiss her strangely mottled cheek. 'Here, let me pull the clothes over you.'

He settled her body in under the blankets and folded them back neatly from her face. 'I'm sorry,' he said. He smoothed the dark hair back from her forehead. 'You're exhausted. You need to sleep.' He brushed tears away with his sleeve. She was so very quiet, so unnaturally quiet. He bent to listen. 'You're holding your breath. You're doing it on purpose to punish me. You're not asleep at all.'

He lay down on the bed and put his arm around her, his face pressed to the back of her head. 'I'm sorry I hurt your poor head. I didn't mean it.' He kissed her hair and ran his fingers lightly over her scalp. 'See, it was only a little knock – no lump, no bleeding. We'll lie here a while, until you feel better. Just one word to tell me you're all right. Don't be like that. One more day now and we'll be off to start a new life – the two of us – alone – together, always. Why don't you say something?'

He got off the bed and settled the blankets around her. 'I'm going back to the house now. She mustn't know anything about us. She must go on thinking she won. You rest here until I come back in the morning. You'll be all right, I promise you. A little knock, hardly loud enough to call a snail out of his shell. Oh, my God! What's wrong? Why aren't you moving? Why aren't you breathing?'

He went down the stairs in a distracted state. She could not slip away and leave him like that. She was only shamming. She had fainted and when she came to she would need him there. Her cheek had been warm. He stood in indecision, then turned and ran back upstairs.

She was lying as he had left her, her dark hair spread on the white pillow. He touched her face. The need to possess her was irresistible. He threw back the blankets, baring her in slow reverence, then took off his clothes and got in beside her, exulting in her unresisting compliance.

Afterwards he lay with her chilling corpse in his arms and cried for himself in his loneliness, and felt a growing anger at her easy abandonment and betrayal.

He got out of bed and dressed. He took blankets from a press and spread them over her, then took her cold feet in his hands, kissed them, blew warm breath on them and carefully covered them. He found more blankets in a bedroom and piled them on top of her. He laid his lips to her icy forehead, then went downstairs and walked out into the starlight, leaving the door open behind him. His feet crunched across the frozen gravel and a thin wind bustled him into the avenue of pines. He looked back and saw the hallway and the upstairs window warm with light, before he reversed the car between the trees and drove back to town.

The phone rang as he walked into the hall. He lifted it and spoke. There was a long silence and then the line went dead. He put the receiver on the table and went upstairs. His wife's voice and the sound of her hands beating on the door came from the bedroom. He turned the key in the lock. She ran past him down the stairs and lifted the phone.

'Wrong number,' he said. 'Who were you expecting to call at this hour?'

She replaced the receiver and went slowly down the hall to the kitchen.

'I want you to know,' he shouted, 'that if anything happens to that child, I'll hold you personally responsible.'

TWENTY-ONE

Hugh came out of the phone box and pulled up his collar against the icy gash of wind. The cuts on his lips and nose stung. His face was puffed and swollen. He thought, from the dull ache, that his nose might be broken. The man was mad to loose off shots at him like that. He had crouched among the pines and heard pellets whine overhead and thud into tree trunks all about him. Ennis had stalked him ruthlessly, with intent to kill. How long had he lain there by the side of the road, where he had fallen from his bicycle in a fit of shivering? Ten minutes? Half an hour?

The man was a pathological liar. Fact and fantasy merged in his mind and flowed in a single stream from his tongue. No father in his senses would confess to such a thing if it were true. But that was the point, that was what sent icicles of doubt shivering through him. Ennis was not sane.

He would not ask her. It was best to forget the Ennises and their tangled lives. Things had always been simple for him. There was only his mother and himself and the memory of a loving father. Eugene was probably still in town. He could be home in an hour. His mother would be waiting. There would be mass in the crisp white morning, full of bell-sound, his neighbours all around him in the little country chapel. Afterwards he would walk through the coarsely stiffened fields and hear the hooves of horses in the lanes ring like iron. And all the time he would wonder about her and have no peace.

He spent what seemed an age in a phone box, trying to get through to Mrs Ennis. The first time he dialled, the phone rang once and the connection was broken. He dialled again and listened to it ring. He was about to give up and risk a direct approach to the house when the receiver was lifted and he recognised the voice of Ennis. He hung up. Where was Mrs Ennis? Why had she not answered earlier?

If Ennis was at home, Mary was alone at Gortnaheensha. Resolutely he turned his bicycle again towards the coast road. Now was the time to help her.

He would not put the question to her. It had to be true. Ennis was abusing her. What else would explain her desperation, the claustrophobic atmosphere of the house, the air of tension and unease, the currents of discord between him and his wife?

On his left the water was solid and full, its metallic surface gathering and throwing back the subdued moonlight. Where it met the sloping sea wall, its edge was roughened with rime. There was no sound except for the whistle of wind through breaches in the wall and the creak and strain of the bicycle chain.

The road turned in from the sea and he saw the lights of Gortnaheensha through the trees to his right. Behind it, the land rose towards Torc Head, sheltering the house from the full force of the Atlantic. The bicycle slid under him as he swung into the drive. He got off and approached the house on foot, and was surprised to see the front door open and the hallway brightly lit.

Ennis would never leave the house like this. There was something wrong. The ladder had been taken away from the wall. He stood and listened. There was no sound from the house. He left the bicycle behind a tree and approached circumspectly. Light splintered on broken glass. He looked up and saw the jagged windowpane. Had Mary escaped down the ladder?

He edged into the hall and stood listening. There was no sound anywhere. If Mary was still up there, his prime concern must be to get her to safety. At the top of the stairs he stood to listen again. The door of Mary's room was open. It was so like a baited trap that he hesitated a long time before entering. He half expected Ennis to come at him with a rush out of nowhere.

'Mary,' he whispered, but there was no answer. The bed was piled with blankets – far too many blankets. No face or head was visible. He stepped into the room, one eye on the corridor. 'Mary,' he called again in a louder voice.

The stillness was unnatural. He tiptoed to the bed. He saw a lock of hair.

'Mary!' he cried.

He pulled back the blankets.

'My God!' His voice trembled; he felt ill. He saw her bruised neck and laid his hand on her frozen forehead. 'She's dead.'

He sank into a kneeling position by the bed. Whimpering and faltering, stopping after every other word, he began to recite the act of contrition. Then, finding her hand and letting his tears fall unchecked, he tried to warm it between his own, massaging the rigid fingers, persuading himself that they were becoming a little more pliable, that he could feel warmth and life returning.

He was still holding it when he heard voices in the hall and footsteps on the stairs. In sudden panic he replaced her hand under the sheet, adjusted the blankets and stood up. Then Sergeant Evans and Garda Cloonan were in the room and he was babbling to them about how he had found her.

Sergeant Evans lifted the blankets, looked at her briefly and sent Garda Cloonan downstairs to phone.

'You'd better sit down,' he said.

Mrs Ennis sat in the kitchen, wondering where Dolan was and why there was no phone call. It was a quarter to midnight – more than an hour after her husband's return. Dare she phone the Dunraven Arms? Supposing he heard her? She had betrayed Mary once already. The only way she could help was to be patient, to wait for her call, to act normally – go to bed. But if she went to bed she might miss the call. In this state of indecision she went upstairs. Leaving the door ajar, she put on her dressing gown over her clothes and knelt beside the bed. She said her usual night prayers and then began the rosary.

Her nodding head came alert with a jerk as the phone rang shrilly. She shook herself and got to her feet. Her left leg was numb. She hobbled to the door in time to hear the voice of her husband in the hall below.

'That's for me,' she began, but fell silent as she heard

his sharp exclamation and then the terse, interrogative monosyllables.

'What is it?' she said, as he laid down the receiver. 'Who was that?'

He turned and looked up the stairwell. Even by the dim light of the hall she could see that his face was strained, bloodless. He made no answer, but stood there, letting his hands sag.

'What's wrong?' She ran down to confront him. 'Who were you talking to?'

'Sergeant Evans,' he said without looking at her. 'I have to go out. Trouble – at Gortnaheensha. They've caught somebody – breaking in.' He turned to go.

'Nothing about . . . ? No mention of . . . Mary?' she asked, feeling faint.

'What's Mary got to do with Gortnaheensha?' He turned on her savagely and caught her wrist. 'You sent her out there? Is that what you're telling me? By God, if any harm comes to her, I'll kill you.' He threw on his overcoat and grabbed the car keys from the hall stand.

She watched him rush out, her mind a confusion of fears. If only she knew what was happening! If only she knew where Mary was and whether she was safe! Was it Dolan they had caught? If it was, wouldn't he have said so? She looked at the phone, mute on its stand, and willed it to ring again. She sat on the stairs, her rosary beads twined in her fingers, waiting.

What had happened? Perhaps the guards were still there. She picked up the phone and dialled Gortnaheensha. The number came to her unbidden, like a memory of childhood. She heard the phone ring at the other end. She listened to it ringing for a long time and was on the point of hanging up when the receiver was lifted and a man's voice answered.

'Is that . . . ? Would that be . . . the gardaí?' Mrs Ennis asked tentatively.

'Who's speaking?' The voice had a surprised, cautious note.

'Is that Gortnaheensha?'

'Yes. Who's that?'

'This is Mrs Ennis speaking.'

'I'm sorry, ma'am.' The voice was respectful. 'Garda Cloonan here.'

'Is there . . . something wrong . . . out there?'

There was a long pause before Garda Cloonan spoke. 'Wasn't the sergeant on to you, ma'am? He left here – it must be – half an hour ago.'

'He was talking to my husband.'

'The priest and the doctor have come and gone,' Cloonan said. 'Everything that could be done has been done. I'm sorry for your trouble, ma'am. I really am.'

Mrs Ennis groped for the chair beside the hall table and sat down. When she tried to speak, her mouth was dry and the words were hard in coming. 'Please . . . tell me . . . what's happened.'

'Didn't the sergeant tell you, ma'am? Didn't your husband tell you?'

'Nobody told me anything. The sergeant phoned my husband and he went out. That's all I know.'

There was a long hesitation at the other end again.

'Are you there?' she asked.

'I'm sorry, ma'am,' Cloonan said awkwardly. 'I shouldn't have been talking to you. The sergeant said I wasn't to talk to anyone. You'll have to speak to him.

Would you like me to get him to ring you?'

'It's Mary,' she said in an expressionless voice.

'I'm sorry, ma'am. If you hang up now, I'll ring the sergeant and he'll tell you everything.'

She heard the click as the receiver was replaced and, like someone in a dream, laid down the phone. Five minutes passed before it rang again. She stared at it, unwilling or unable to reach out for it. It went silent for a minute and started again. She lifted it and, trembling, held it to her ear.

'Sergeant Evans here, Mrs Ennis. I'm afraid I've some very bad news for you. I thought Mr Ennis would have told you.'

'It's Mary,' she said. 'Isn't it?'

'I'm afraid, Mrs Ennis, that your daughter is . . . dead. I'm sorry.'

'Dead? Mary dead?'

'I'm afraid so.'

'My God!' she groaned, as the full horror of it struck her. 'My husband!'

'Yes, poor man,' the sergeant said compassionately. 'I'm afraid it's been a dreadful shock for him. He's here at the station. Would you like a word with him?'

Ennis was drinking tea in a bleak little room, unfurnished except for a table, three chairs and a grey filing cabinet. He looked up as the sergeant returned and passed his hand wearily across his grizzly stubbled chin.

'That was unfortunate,' the sergeant said, closing the door, 'your wife ringing Gortnaheensha like that. It appears she didn't know?' He finished with a question rather than a statement and stood waiting.

Ennis clasped and unclasped his hands before him on the table. 'I wanted to be sure – to have all the facts. There could have been . . . a mistake.'

'Unfortunately,' the sergeant said, 'there has been no mistake. Your wife was concerned about you. I asked her if she'd like to talk to you, but she was too distraught and hung up. Would you like to ring her?'

Ennis shook his head and made a despairing gesture with his hands.

'I didn't say anything about this fellow Dolan, or how it happened,' the sergeant continued. 'One shock was enough for the moment. Maybe you'd tell her later? I'll talk to her myself when I'm finished here.'

'She could never see bad in that fellow,' Ennis said bleakly. 'Mary was terrified of him.'

'You say you took the girl out to Gortnaheensha to protect her from him?'

'Yes. The place was ours one time, as you know. She'd feel safe there.'

'How did you get in?'

'We had an arrangement. The priests left the keys with us. People who came to stay collected them and left them back before they went.'

'Wouldn't she be frightened on her own in an old deserted house like that?'

'She knew the place well. She grew up there as a child. She'd often been out since on weekend retreats with her class. She wasn't afraid.'

'How did Dolan get to know where she was?'

'He was hanging about all evening. He must have seen us and . . . ' He buried his face in his hands.

'Here's a question,' the sergeant said. 'You saw Dolan snooping around and scared him off. After that you came back to town. Why did you come back? Why didn't you stay with Mary or take her home with you?'

'I didn't think there was any need. I didn't think he'd come back. It was only later that I got to worrying.'

'Yes, yes, of course. So you rang the station?'

'Yes.' Ennis nodded wearily. The thing was like a nightmare, a circular horror from which he had tried to wake and couldn't. The knowledge that he couldn't was part of the nightmare. Why was he going through this charade? What difference did it make who was responsible? Mary was dead. She was gone and he was alone.

Sergeant Evans took a watch out of his pocket. 'Do you recognise this?'

'Mary's watch. Of course I recognise it. I gave it to her.'

'Was she wearing it today?' He glanced at the time. 'I mean yesterday?'

'She never took it off. It's an expensive watch.'

'I can see that,' the sergeant said. 'I'm afraid we'll have to hold it as evidence. It appears that Garda Cloonan found it in Dolan's pocket. He claimed your daughter gave it to him.'

'That's a lie.'

The sergeant nodded. Ennis stared in silence at the table-top. There were black stains, like shallow craters, indented into it. They looked like cigarette burns. It seemed important to keep his mind focused on them. What, he wondered, was he going to do with the rest of his life?

'Now,' the sergeant said kindly, 'I know you'll be worried about Mrs Ennis alone in the house, and anxious to get back to her. Garda Cloonan will drive you home.'

'No need for that.' Ennis shook his head. 'I can look after myself.'

It seemed to Hugh that he had been sitting there for hours. His head sagged and he found it hard to keep his eyes open. When Sergeant Evans came back, he was carrying a cup of tea, which he pushed across the table.

'Now, why don't you tell the truth?' he coaxed.

'Ask Mr Ennis that question,' Hugh muttered.

'Are you accusing the man of killing his own daughter?'

'If it wasn't me, it must have been him – and I know it wasn't me.'

'You won't help yourself by accusing James Ennis. Everybody knows he thought the world of that girl. What motive could he possibly have?'

'I don't know. All I know is that he kept her locked in like a prisoner. Why did he do a thing like that? You ask him. Talk to Mrs Ennis.'

'I intend to.'

'Ask her where Mary was really going – and why. Ask her –'

'You don't have to teach me my job,' the sergeant cut him off angrily.

'No, sir,' Hugh said humbly. 'All I wanted to say was that Mrs Ennis knows why I was out in Gortnaheensha. She gave me the key. She sent me there.'

'She sent you there! For what purpose?'

'To see if Mary was there and to get her out if she was.'

'What did you know about the domestic affairs of the Ennises?'

'I knew that Mary was going off to Dublin – she told

me. When I saw him driving her out the coast road, I thought it odd and told Mrs Ennis. They were arguing. It looked as if he was taking her against her will.'

'Don't speculate; keep to the facts,' the sergeant said severely.

'It's a fact that they were arguing. It's a fact that he took her out there. It's a fact that he kept her locked up – even at home.'

'So what? He kept her in. He may, occasionally, have locked her up. In my book a father has that right; she was still a minor. The relationship between a father and his daughter is a very special thing, something you'd know nothing about. So don't let me hear any more of this malicious nonsense about her father. It won't stand well with you in court. No jury is going to have any sympathy –'

'You seem to have me condemned before you've looked into the thing at all,' Hugh protested desperately.

'What I'm saying is that there's a case to answer and you'd better answer it.'

'I am answering it,' Hugh said. 'But you won't believe me. I told you he had her locked up in Gortnaheensha. I did my best to help her. I got into the hall, but I couldn't open the other door. I was trying the window when he came along and attacked me. When I went back later, all the doors were open and the lights were on. There was no sign of him or the gun –'

'What gun?'

'I told you, he tried to kill me. The doors were open. I went upstairs and there she was, her skin cold and white. I still can't believe she's . . . dead.' He lowered his head and began to heave.

'She's dead all right,' the sergeant said brutally, 'and

you killed her.'

'Why would I harm her?' Hugh sobbed. 'Mary of all people!'

TWENTY-TWO

. . . Garda authorities are treating as murder the death of a sixteen-year-old girl near Tubberfulla. The body was found by members of the force who went to the scene in response to a phone call. The discovery was made in an upstairs bedroom of a local mansion, the property of the Patrician fathers, a missionary order with headquarters in Dublin. . .

Mrs Ennis sat in the cold light of a December morning, staring at the radio. Her face was blank, washed clean of expression, anaesthetised by shock. These were the kind of things that happened to other people, in other places. They had no reality, apart from a flicker of half-life in the imagination.

Garda sources reveal that death was caused by strangulation. The name of the murdered girl is being withheld until the next of kin have been informed. A young man is helping the gardaí with their inquiries . . .

That was Mary the newsreader was talking about in his cold, dispassionate way. That was her daughter.

So, poor Hugh was helping them with their inquiries, was he? She sat at the scrubbed deal table, covering her face with her hands. She wondered where *he* was, what he was doing, what he felt about his daughter now.

She huddled close to the stove. The frost of the night had entered into her and she felt that she would never be warm again. Her rosary beads kept circling through her fingers. There was comfort in them, but there was no prayer. Her attempts at prayer were just a jumble of words that circulated in her head.

She blamed herself. Out in Gortnaheensha Mary was lying dead. It was her fault. She had sent her through that kitchen door to her death. She had sent her to her death a long time ago, when, through fear of scandal, she had given her husband's crime the seal of her silence. Everything had followed from that.

She sat waiting for Sergeant Evans. She would make a full confession. There was no punishment that the law had devised for people like her. She would never again feel free of guilt. How could she? Mary was dead and there could be no undoing that.

Morning came in greyly and found her still sitting there. She was unaware of it until the sound of the doorbell penetrated her consciousness. It came from a great distance, cutting through her grief. She didn't want to see anyone. Perhaps if she did nothing, they'd go away. The bell continued to ring.

Sergeant Evans, looking tired and pinched in his blue overcoat, was standing on the doorstep with Mary's bag in his hand. 'Sorry to disturb you so early,' he said softly. 'I wonder if I could have a word.'

She opened the door and beckoned him in. He followed

her down the passage into the kitchen. He laid the bag on the table, pulled off his gloves and held out his hand.

'My condolences,' he said. 'I'm sorry to be here on such an errand.'

She took his hand without speaking and nodded her head.

'Unfortunately,' he continued, 'it's my duty to ask questions and to look for answers. It isn't easy being a policeman in circumstances like these. I won't detain you very long, I promise you. I'd like you to check through your daughter's bag here, to see if anything is missing – and to answer a few questions.'

'How did it . . . happen?' she asked. 'I've been sitting here all night, knowing nothing except that she was dead.'

'But your husband? Didn't he tell you when he came back?'

'He didn't come back. All I know is what I've just heard on the radio.'

'Your daughter was strangled. Mercifully it must have been quick. There was very little sign of a struggle. Do you know anybody who'd want to do a thing like that to her? Is there anything you can tell us?'

'Did you talk to my husband?' she asked sharply.

'Yes. He was very helpful, poor man. It was a great shock to him. There was . . . something else . . . I'm afraid. We have reason to believe that she – this will distress you, but, according to the doctor's preliminary report – she may have been sexually assaulted.'

Mrs Ennis bowed her head and subsided into a chair.

'I'm sorry,' Sergeant Evans said.

She nodded. Sexual assault was nothing new to her. There could be no surprise in that. 'What did my husband say about it?'

The sergeant looked at her as if he thought it an odd sort of question. 'He doesn't know yet. We weren't sure at the time. The doctor had only made a summary examination and the poor man was so distressed – I've never seen anybody so distressed – that I thought it could wait a little longer.'

It was painful to have to listen to the sergeant in his blundering, well-meaning way. For all his confident manner, he was hopelessly adrift.

'We're holding young Dolan for further questioning. Your husband has no doubts about his guilt. It seems to me that the evidence against him is overwhelming. But before we come to that, I want you to check through this bag and tell me if what's in it belongs to your daughter.'

'Hugh Dolan had nothing to do with it,' she said. 'I'm sure of that.'

'How can you be sure,' the sergeant asked, as he watched her spill out the contents of the bag on the table, 'when you know nothing of the circumstances? I must tell you we found him standing beside the body.'

The sight of Mary's things upset her. He watched her pick up a hair slide with a red butterfly on it and turn away to hide her grief. 'Where did you get this?' she whispered.

'I believe your daughter was wearing it.'

He watched in puzzlement as she lifted the top of the stove and threw the slide into the fire, crying, 'The obscenity of it!'

When she recovered she said, 'Talk to my husband. He'll be able to answer all your questions.'

'What do you mean? What should I ask him?'

Mrs Ennis picked up the diary that had tumbled out of

the bag and held it to her breast. 'You should ask him just one question,' she said passionately. 'Ask him why he raped and murdered his own daughter.'

'Your husband?'

'Yes,' she said firmly through her tears. 'My husband.'

Leaving the barracks, he drove out to Gortnaheensha, obsessed with the idea of having one last look at her before she was taken away for ever.

When he came to the gate, he saw the Garda car and the ambulance on the gravel. The house was brightly lit. He drove past, switched off the engine, got out and walked back. He saw the doors of the ambulance being closed. Then he heard the engine start up and the crisp bite of tyres on gravel. The headlights came probing towards him. He stood behind the pier and watched the ambulance turn in the direction of town. When he looked back to the house, it was no longer visible and the Garda car was speeding towards him, zipping up the darkness behind it.

They would take her to the mortuary in the hospital, where she would lie on a cold slab and the state pathologist would examine her. He would throw back the sheet carelessly and turn her about, this way and that, as if she was so much carrion. The newspapers would flaunt headlines, screaming murder and rape. *She* might talk, and then it would be incest, the unnatural crime. But what, he asked himself, could be more natural than life drawing strength from its own source.

He went back to the car and sat in. His eyes, accustomed to the darkness, looked out over the scrub and marshland that bordered Gortnaheensha. He knew the ground well, had shot over it many times in pursuit of teal and widgeon. Down to the left was a piece of tidal swamp where he had lain in the reeds at twilight, awaiting the return of mallard.

He laid his forehead on the wheel and cried – not for her, because she was safe – but for himself in his loneliness. He would never find her again. At best there would be illusions of her, tiny glimpses to startle and excite – the scent of a hand, the curve of an eyelash, to set him searching with wildly beating heart. There would be echoes of her voice on the summer wind. He would feel her in the warmth of the sun, stirring up desires and harrowing his flesh with cruel fingernails.

He sat until the dark paled into a frosty dawn. When a tinge of lemon stained the horizon, he drove back to town. There was no purpose in his driving. What did it matter where he went? He drove through streets that had a somnolent, sabbath air, with a few elderly people going to early mass. Habit brought him along the Killawley Road. He drove by without a glance. What if there was unfinished business in that house? Her best punishment was to be left there to carry the burden alone.

He was crossing the bridge when he saw Dolan cycling towards him, a scarf covering the lower part of his face. He braked, let down the window and shouted. Dolan pulled up with one foot on the ground. He reached for the shotgun beside him, pushed out the barrel and drew back the hammers. Lifting the gun to his cheek, he took a sighting. Dolan stared at him, mesmerised. He curled his finger round the trigger and felt it go tense. Dolan balanced there, unable to move. The bastard's life was in his hands.

His finger was tightening to the point of release when he jerked the barrel upwards and relaxed the muscles of his trigger finger. What the hell had Dolan to do with it, anyway? He eased back the hammers and drew in the gun. He shook himself, like a man waking from a dream, and drove on out the coast road.

He turned right and drove uphill, until he reached an open place, where he parked and sat looking out over the frost-bound town. Down where the trees loomed dark, at the other side of Paupers' Acre, was the field where it had happened. He had often lain there afterwards, waiting for her return. He had conceived the notion that, if he concentrated deeply enough, he would draw her back. Sometimes at twilight, when the crows were tumultuous overhead and shadows took on reality in the half-light, he had dim sightings of her like a wraith in a mist and felt his heart leap.

He got out of the car, taking the shotgun with him, and crossed into Paupers' Acre, rasping through coarse grass. He came out by the broken wall into Sullivan's Limbo, a rectangle with a single grave, topped by a crude iron cross, and climbed into the field beyond. The place was somewhere near. He crossed into another field, narrow as a coffin, that ran parallel with the main configuration of the town, and searched frantically for familiar landmarks. He climbed the ditch into the next field – and there it was. He stood looking at his past. His mind burned with a scalding tenderness as the years fell away. There was the very spot where he had seen her, lying in the same sun that gleamed intermittently now in the pale dawn.

There was no feeling of coming to the end of a long pilgrimage – nothing but the bite of a raw morning, the grass shackled in frost, the low sky pregnant with snow. There was nothing here for him, no more than anywhere else.

Twice she had slipped away. Now she was out there, waiting. Life was the only barrier between them. At best life was no more than a window, through which you caught glimpses of glory. To see the full picture you had to break the glass.

He removed the lace from his boot, looped it round the trigger, and tied the loose ends in a knot. If he slipped his foot into the noose, as into a stirrup, all he had to do was extend his leg.

He closed his eyes to the December light and retired deep within himself. He shut from his mind the frozen earth on which he sat. He locked his ears against the whisper of wind. He would wash the memory of the world from his mind and let her spirit pour in. To entice her, he cast off his clothes. When he was naked, he began to prepare himself for her, holding his foot bent to the stirrup, while he teased visions of her out of his flesh.

The first intimation of her rippled his mind like sunshine. She was a potentiality. She was a possibility. She was there. She was on the other side of the glass. With life spurting from him, he hurled himself towards her. The glass shattered in a million fragments and the last image on his exploding retina was blood, falling like rain.